DESCENDENT OF SALEM

Robert James

Tell-Tale Publishing Group, LLC
Swartz Creek, MI 48737

Printed in the United States of America

CHAPTER ONE

Dylan sat alone in the cemetery and waited for his wife. He'd seen Mary so many times since she died he didn't care anymore about what was real, what was possible. She went away and never said goodbye, and that left Dylan to relive his loss, searching for answers he'd never find. Their conversations helped Dylan escape the pain, to break free from the crushing weight of his emptiness, and he needed her tonight – to touch her, kiss her – to tell her his life was hell without her.

"Hello, my love."

The warm embrace of Mary's voice brushed past his ears and she materialized in front of him. She giggled and walked the short distance from her tombstone to where he sat under the tree. Her black hair fell across her shoulders and her blue eyes sparkled with the light of the moon.

"Where have you been my whole life?" she kicked his leg with her bare foot.

Dylan smiled.

Those were the first words Mary had ever said to him, the words that started the aimless but profound conversation that came out of their chance encounter. The details were fuzzy – he recalled the warmth of the sun, the park, the ducks on the pond – but the connection he felt that day still beat strong in his heart.

Mary was his forever, his soulmate.

"I miss you."

"You remember that day, don't you?"

"Of course," Dylan said. "I remember the way you looked, the way your eyes lit up your entire face." Dylan kissed the back of Mary's hand and savored the imaginary warmth of her skin against his lips. "Mostly, I just remember how I felt. That was the day I became yours."

"You'll always be mine," Mary said.

The folds of her black gown billowed gently as she held Dylan's shoulders, straddled his thighs and settled into his lap. He could almost smell the lavender in the gentle curls of her black hair as her tongue tickled his earlobe and her lips found his cheek. They were cold, just a reminder of what was, but Dylan's heart pounded just the same, and he matched the gentle rhythm of her hips. As his body responded to her touch, he pictured the warmth of his flesh transferring to Mary through their embrace, giving her life, making her whole again.

"I wish you were still here," he said.

"I am here, silly." Mary kissed his neck and ran her fingers through his thick black hair. "I'll always be here, just for you," she whispered.

"But it's not the same," Dylan said, "I wish I was with you. I wish..." He wanted tonight to be different, but his emotions always led him to the same place. "Why?" He asked. "Why did you do it, Mary?"

Her body stiffened.

"It doesn't really matter, does it? What's important is that you'll always be mine." She ran her finger down his nose and tapped it playfully. "You want to be mine forever, don't you?"

"Of course."

"Then why haven't you answered my question?" Mary's voice turned to ice. "Where have you been my whole life? I know where I've been." She pulled a clump of dirt from her hair and threw it at his face. "But where exactly have you been lately?"

The warm glow that surrounded Dylan's memories was replaced by the dark, damp reality of the cemetery. Mary's hair became a tangled mess, her face and neck bruised, like the night he found her in the basement.

"I asked you a question, you son of a bitch. You think I don't know about her? What's her name, Dylan? Are you fucking her?" Mary's lifeless, unblinking eyes stared at him accusingly and she grabbed him by the throat. "I lie here all day waiting for you, and you're off fucking some slut, aren't you?" She slammed the back of his head against the trunk of the tree. "I know you're fucking her, Dylan!"

Dylan broke free from Mary's embrace and scrambled to his feet. Their link severed, she disappeared. He took a long pull from his flask, then walked over to Mary's headstone and lay down in the fledgling grass. He reached up and traced the outline of her name across the cool marble slab with his left ring finger. A tear rolled out the corner of his eye and mingled with the earth beneath his cheek.

Longing for an imperfect past, Dylan Ward cried himself to sleep.

***

Anne stopped at the end of the footbridge that joined Pine Island to Leahy Cay and checked the contents of her basket one final time. Satisfied, she closed the lid and set off into the forest. The path was worn to dirt from her countless excursions, and even without the light of the full moon, she could easily find her way to the top of the hill. The soil had a rich, sharp smell tonight, blanketed by the moist leaves of the hardwood forest surrounding her. Pine Island was aptly named, but her grandfather's island – Leahy Cay would always be her grandfather's island – was mainly oak, ash and birch, with a few gnarly old apple trees mixed in.

Even now, twelve years since he passed, her head was flooded with memories, especially in the stones at the top of the hill. As a green witch, Anne practiced her craft throughout the year, but here on the hill, she felt a special connection that she didn't experience anywhere else. Her craft was consistent, but the results were always amplified, more tangible. Her grandfather always denied experiencing it, but he encouraged her to spend time on the hill, and explore what she felt.

The raspberry bushes called to her as she walked by, so she stopped and gathered a handful and put them into her basket. She popped one in her mouth and was transported back to her childhood. She remembered the gentle strength of her grandfather's hand on her shoulder and the minty smokiness of his breath. She could hear his voice; *when they're ready, they'll basically fall into your hand,* he told her. *Never take them from the bush, let them give themselves to you.*

When she was a child, Anne used to play on the hill, inspired by the remains of the stone circle. She created whole worlds filled with fantastic characters and epic adventures. The summer of her eighth birthday, Anne's grandfather began to teach her the true significance of the island, the hill, and the stones. He was the one that taught her about witchcraft, how to honor the earth, to tap into the energy of the elements and to maintain balance in her life. That was what tonight was for: to honor his wisdom, to reconnect with the spirit of the island, and officially welcome another summer.

Anne paused as she reached the top of the hill, resting under the towering oak tree that spread its canopy over the large rocks. The stones were more or less in a circle, but were strewn around, like scattered dominoes. The oak tree had grown out of the largest stone – the one with a shallow depression in the top that faced east, out over Lake Huron – its trunk enveloping and growing around the large boulder. A few of its lower branches spread out like enormous vines, running along the ground and creating small natural pockets that seemed tailor made to support Anne's frame. She closed her eyes and grounded herself, visualizing her body entering the soil and mingling with the roots of the ancient tree. After a few minutes of measured breathing, she adjusted her salt-and-pepper ponytail and entered the stone circle. She placed her basket in the center, then emptied its contents before placing a white linen cloth over it.

She started with four candles, placing one on top of a stone at each of the cardinal points, with the fourth in the small depression in the capstone. She put a white spell candle on the cloth next to an oak leaf, then invoked each element – earth, air, fire, and water – before lighting its respective candle.

She knelt in front of her makeshift altar and opened a worn leather journal – her grandfather's grimoire – and flipped to a page she had bookmarked. She didn't need the book to remember the spell but seeing his scribbles next to hers in the margins comforted her. Toward the back of the book, he had catalogued the celestial markers that were built into the hill, noting the appropriate moon phase and sun position for the ceremonies associated with the wheel of the year. Anne checked the notes for the summer solstice one final time and then began.

"I invite you, my guardian, to join me on this special night. I request your presence as I celebrate your continued blessings, honor your ancient wisdom and strength, and prepare for our journey back into the darkness."

Anne lit the white candle on the altar and the air around her began to hum with the energy of her intentions. It called to her like a faint whisper from the far reaches of her mind, pulling her inward. She watched the flame of the candle as it danced on the currents of the summer wind, took a deep breath and exhaled slowly. Anne closed her eyes and focused on the warmth creeping down her limbs and across her chest.

There you are, she thought.

Anne shifted her attention from the rhythmic cadence of her breath to the energy gently pulling her deeper into her mind. She followed the trail into her subconscious and pictured herself, kneeling alone in the stones beneath the oak tree, while the bright light washed over her. A gentle breeze rustled the leaves of the tree, stirring up the scent of the forest, and she felt the warm pulse radiating out from her body and into the soil.

Then, slowly, the gentle thump in her ears was replaced by a voice. It started as a faint whisper, familiar and inviting, and it reminded Anne of her grandfather's gravely tone. As the words became more distinct, the pitch changed, and she knew it was someone else. It was a voice that she didn't know but had heard a thousand times before.

'This is for you,' he said.

The words seemed to come from right over her shoulder in the stone circle. She opened her eyes and scanned the forest, but there was nobody there.

***

Dylan awoke the next morning to the sound of birds. Their chirping, and the inevitable creep of daylight, gave life to the inherent calm of the cemetery. Sleeping on the ground was not kind to Dylan's thirty-two-year-old frame. His back ached and his shoulder sent a sharp protest of pain down his arm. He got to his feet, smiled at Mary's tombstone and walked away. His legs were especially sore today, and he scuffed the dirt every third step or so, sending pebbles knocking down the path ahead of him. He wasn't going to sneak up on anyone, but that's why Dylan liked it here.

He was always alone in the cemetery.

To his left were some of the older headstones. Many were falling over, their letters worn from nearly 150 years of exposure to wind, rain, snow and ice. One always got his attention. It looked like an ancient book, with two round pages opened to the world. *Constance and Margaret, aged 6 and 8 years,* it read. Dylan often wondered what sort of disease or family tragedy had taken these two children and their mother, Abigail, on the same day back in 1846. Somehow, he felt connected to them through his own darkness, the common thread of their pain bridging time and space.

Ahead, there was a crossroads, where four paths converged at a white marble memorial from the Civil War. A lone Union soldier leaned against a musket and looked out over the grass. As he walked past the soldier and approached the fence, he noticed his friend Kyle standing in the street. He leaned against the passenger side door of his red pickup truck, arms folded, a thermos of coffee and two mugs next to him.

"Dylan Ward, *Esquire*," he said. "Thought I might find you here."

Kyle liked to use the honorific with an *'a lot of fucking good that's done you'* tone in his voice. He was entirely self-made, working in restaurants and taking odd jobs to help pay for his culinary classes at the local community college. When Dylan's world imploded, and he couldn't pay his bills, Kyle gave him a job at his restaurant, but it wasn't a free ride. Dylan would never admit it to his best friend, but he had never worked so hard in his life.

"You know, wearing all black doesn't make you a ninja," Kyle said. "FYI, the white toes on those black Converse sneakers aren't doing you any favors. I'm surprised someone hasn't called the cops on you after all these months."

Dylan vaulted to the grass outside the cemetery and walked over to the truck without responding. He wiped his hands on the back of his black jeans, smoothed his black t-shirt with mock embellishment, and took the mug from Kyle's outstretched hand.

"Did you see her again?" Kyle asked.

"Yep," Dylan said and sipped his coffee. "I can't explain it, but it's like she's really there. When I come to the cemetery, I just wait, and she shows up. When she talks, I hear her voice. When she touches me..." Dylan looked away from his friend and took another sip from his mug.

"Look buddy," Kyle said, "I'm not going to rehash everything you went through. Even on the good days, your life was a roller coaster with Mary at the very end. I get it. But look," he scratched his chin with his thumb, choosing his words. "The way she decided to say good-bye has left you in a tailspin for the last ten months, and I feel like you're losing your grip lately."

"I'm alright," Dylan said. "Trust me, I'm fine."

"Yeah, well, you need to start living for you," Kyle said and put his hand on Dylan's shoulder. "When was the last time you spent some quality time with Jillian?"

Jillian was a recently divorced mother of three, and by *'quality time'* he meant *'fucked.'* Kyle's wife Edy had introduced her to Dylan at a cookout, thinking they would share a connection of sexual convenience after a long night of drinking, but he wasn't ready to move on from Mary. He'd tried to avoid her ever since.

"She's great and all," Dylan said, "but I'm just not ready for a commitment yet."

"Whoa, who said anything about commitment?" Kyle retorted. "From what Edy tells me, she's not looking for anything serious either, so why not have some fun? Do you know how many guys would love to have a friend like that?"

"It's not that simple," Dylan said. "Mary says things, like she's watching me or something, like she knows what I'm doing. It's – it's just...."

"Oh, for fuck's sake," Kyle said. "That shit is all in your head, buddy. I know you're not into therapy, but have you thought about meditation, or something else like that? You need to do something, Dylan. *I* need you to do something." Kyle took a sip of his coffee and exhaled. "I'm getting complaints from customers, and I can't have you staring off into space and reeking of booze when you take an order from a family of six, you get me?"

Dylan's face flushed and he took a sip of coffee. Kyle was right, of course. Dylan's life had become a predictable cliché of misery and melancholy. The road to her death was rocky, but when Mary died the bottom completely fell out of Dylan's life and he simply stopped caring, content to tumble headlong into the darkness.

"If it happens again," Kyle continued, "I'm gonna have to move you to the back of the house."

"Is that why you came here this morning?" Dylan asked.

"Of course," Kyle replied, "you think I came here to watch the sunrise and share a cup of coffee with you? I'm way too busy for that kind of shit."

Kyle started his truck, lowered his window, and pointed at Dylan's mug.

"You done with that?"

"Sure," Dylan said.

He took one last sip, threw the rest on the ground, and handed the mug to his friend.

"I'm off to Reynold's farm to get this week's share. Wanna' join?"

"Why, so I can load everything in the truck, while you and old man Reynolds shoot the shit about the accuracy of the weather predictions in *The Farmer's Almanac*? I don't think so."

"Whatever," Kyle said. "Consider this your first and only warning. I love you man, but– "

"—I know," Dylan interrupted, "it's just business."

"No, dude," Kyle replied, "it's *my* business. I'll see you tonight."

Dylan gave his friend the middle finger and started walking home.

CHAPTER TWO

There was something in the water. Erik Larson didn't know what it was yet, but he knew it shouldn't be hidden at the bottom of Lake Huron. What he saw in the rocks around Pine Island was a game changer, the stuff of television, best-selling books and speaking tours. Out of habit, he checked over his shoulder one more time to see if anyone had followed him. The sun was just breaking the horizon and there were no other boats in sight.

He pushed play on his GoPro, and held it at arm's length, so he was shooting himself against the backdrop of the open lake.

"Hey, guys! If you watch my videos, you already know that I never know what I'm going to find on my adventures, but today – oh, man – today, I'm sharing something beyond amazing with you." Erik focused briefly on the boulders piled up on the shoreline, panned up the cliff to the top of the hill where the remains of the stone circle jutted out from the trees, then quickly framed his face again. "I promise it's way beyond fishing lures, car parts or lost jewelry, and if you're watching this, that means that it's time to share it with the world. You ready? Let's see what's waiting for us in a cave, fifty feet below the surface of Lake Huron. I'm gonna gear up, and I'll see you in the water!"

His air on, his gear in place, Erik hugged the GoPro to his chest, and rolled backwards off the side of the boat, the cold water sending sharp needles across his face. He hovered near the surface, looked down at his destination, and waited for the shock to dissipate. The water was clear, and he could just make out the dark outline of the cave entrance beckoning from fifty feet below. He turned the camera back on and made sure it was recording. He wasn't going to miss anything today.

When he reached the cave, he adjusted his buoyancy, and turned on his dive light. He was deep enough that the sunlight was muted, turning everything a greyish brown. His light gave the world life – well, at least gave it some color – highlighting the reds and greens of the rocks and the black of the zebra mussels that covered them. He grabbed hold of the boulder that covered half of the entrance and aimed his light into the darkness. With a few gentle kicks he glided into the tunnel that led to the main chamber. Spiral patterns, and concentric circles with straight lines radiating out from their centers, covered every inch of the tunnel's surface.

Even though he was just here a few days ago, Erik's pulse still quickened.

As he entered the main chamber, he focused his camera on the large rock in the center of the room. It looked like a bowl, with a shallow depression and more spirals carved into its surface. That was where he had found the crystal sphere that was locked in his safe back home. If he could create enough hype, it should fetch a nice price. There were two cardinal rules in scuba diving: never hold your breath and always dive with a buddy. The first was unavoidable, but Erik found the second to be a hassle. Profits went further when there wasn't somebody asking for their cut.

The wall of the cave was filled with similar markings as the tunnel. It all seemed to be telling a story. Straight lines of different lengths came out from large circles that all converged on two figures that knelt together at the center of the carving. Erik panned slowly across the wall with his camera, making sure he got every detail. His heart pounded and he smiled so wide, his regulator nearly fell out of his mouth.

This was his ticket.

It had to be.

***

Tucked around the corner of the inlet to Pine Island, in a small blue cottage at the end of the lane, Anne scraped obsessively at her blueberry yogurt, trying to coax one last spoonful from the bottom of the container. She'd always been an active child, ran track in high school and had exercised regularly her entire adult life, but her body never seemed to respond to her efforts. Just the same, she tried to make healthy food choices, in case it changed its mind.

She sat at the kitchen table, her robe wrapped loosely around her damp skin, a towel twisted above her head like a giant serving of purple soft serve ice cream. Beyond the footbridge, the open water of Lake Huron glimmered a rich Caribbean blue. Two years ago, Anne decided to walk away from a lucrative career in finance to focus on the parts of her life that she never had time for – exercise, cooking, gardening, sleeping – and this morning she had already run a circuit of her grandfather's island, watered her herbs, and set out the annuals she had just bought in Eagleton, across the bay.

As she sat savoring her yogurt, she caught a glimpse of movement around the rocks leading into the inlet. A boat was making slow but steady progress toward the footbridge that connected to Leahy Cay. Ever since she moved to the island, privacy was Anne's most treasured possession, and she guarded it ruthlessly. The longer Anne was alone, though, the more she struggled with human contact, especially with strangers. It was like her confidence and swagger had been abducted and were being held at an undisclosed location. Anger and isolation were her favorite ways to deal with her blossoming anxiety. Local teenagers trying to get away from their parents and young lovers looking for a private spot sought refuge on her grandfather's island on a regular basis, and they were easy targets for Anne's rage. She always gave them plenty of time to get started. In fact, she prided herself on her uncanny ability to wait until climax was imminent, before jumping out of the bushes to surprise them.

Some people got off stealing lipstick from Wal-Mart.

Anne Leahy stole orgasms.

People didn't always want to comply, and she was trying to decide if she would bring the baseball bat, or her grandfather's shotgun, when she noticed a red flag clipped to the front window of the boat. It had a single white stripe running from corner to corner, the 'diver down' maritime signal warning other boats to keep their distance. That was a first. She'd never seen a scuba diver nearby.

The boat made a slight turn and the stern tapped gently against the footbridge. Anne watched the phantom aquanaut jump out of the boat and tie it down next to her 'Private Dock, No Trespassing' sign. He looked over his shoulder at the house and his eyes caught hers through the kitchen window.

He waved.

Apparently, he wasn't here to sneak around. Anne's breasts peeked out from the loose confines of her robe to stare with her at the mop of blonde hair attached to his chiseled face.

"Shit," Anne whispered.

She jumped to her feet and scurried into the bedroom to get dressed. She threw the robe and towel onto the floor in a heap and rifled through her dresser. There was no time for underwear. She shimmied on a pair of black yoga pants and wiggled into a t-shirt. She tousled her hair, pushed up her breasts with both hands, and gave herself a sideways glance in the mirror.

Anne had always considered her breasts a package deal – they were included at no extra charge with her generous frame – but they made first impressions a constant challenge. Even when she didn't want to, her girls often made a dramatic, and unexpected, appearance. Anne glanced at the front door, cursed, and threw the t-shirt at the wall behind her.

"Calm down," she said to the mirror, inhaling through her nose and exhaling out her mouth.

She put on a ratty, oversized sweatshirt she had been wearing since college, and expertly pulled her wet hair up into a ponytail. With a groan, she padded across the living room and out the front door.

"I won't be long, I promise," the diver said, giving her a quick glance. It was just a passing glance, but it was enough to make her cross her arms protectively across her chest.

"Okay," she replied.

He walked over to her and stopped at a polite distance a few feet away.

"I'm Erik," he said.

"Anne," she replied. She looked down at his boat and hoped he wouldn't notice her cheeks were flushed. "So, what's so interesting down there? I've never seen anyone diving around here before."

"Oh, nothing much. I was just poking around in the rocks," he lied.

"You mean my rocks?" she countered, tucking a few wisps of hair behind her ears.

"Yours? You own that island?" Erik raised an eyebrow and Anne responded with a tight smile. "I'm sorry, I figured it was public land since there was nothing on it. I guess I owe you an apology and a thank you. Although, technically speaking, the shoreline and the bottomlands belong to the people of the great State of Michigan. Either way, I hope you don't mind me blowing a few bubbles down there."

"I don't see any harm in it, I guess," Anne said.

"So, why don't you have a house or something up there?" Erik pointed to the crest of the hill, where what was left of the stone circle looked out over lake. "The view must be awesome."

"I inherited the land from my grandfather," she said. "It just seems right the way it is."

Anne kicked at the ground, polishing the footbridge with her toes.

"It's a bit isolated here, but it must be worth a mint," he said. "If it were me, I'd sell it and live off the interest on some tropical island. Dive by day, drink fruity cocktails by night..." He trailed off, his eyes a million miles away. "Do you mind if I use your bathroom? I usually just go off the side of the boat, but under the circumstances?"

Shit, she thought, *why won't you go away?*

“Follow me,” she said and walked back to the cottage, her arms still folded. When she reached the front porch, she turned and said, “Can you give me a sec? I wasn’t expecting any company today.”

“No problem,” Erik replied.

He stood on the porch and waited.

Anne calmly walked inside, but as soon as the door shut behind her, she sprang into action. She gave the bathroom a once over, retrieved her dirty clothes, wiped down the sink and put out a fresh hand towel. She threw the clothes – and as much clutter as she could fit into her arms – onto the floor of her bedroom and shut the door.

“Thanks for waiting,” she said and opened the front door. “It’s right over there.”

Erik nodded a thank-you, walked into the bathroom and shut the door.

Anne positioned herself in the kitchen, facing the bathroom, and cracked open the pantry door so her grandfather’s shotgun was within reach. It would be just her luck, Michelangelo’s *David* dropping in to use the toilet, but turning out to be an axe murderer.

Anne didn’t owe her financial success to kowtowing to every pretty face that crossed her path, but nonetheless, she was mesmerized by the sound of Erik relieving himself. She held her breath and listened to the hypnotic sound coming from her bathroom, trying to imagine how he looked at that moment. She pictured him through the door, standing there in his tight jeans, smiling at her over his broad shoulders. Was he right-handed or left?

The sound of the toilet flushing brought her back to the reality of her kitchen and she straightened up in anticipation.

“Thanks again,” Erik said. “I’ll get out of your hair.”

He gave her a quick wink and walked out the front door.

“Yeah, sure, no problem,” Anne said, after he was halfway to the footbridge.

She looked at him through the kitchen window as he started his engine and backed away from the dock. He smiled and waved, then sped out of the cove and into the lake.

"Bye...Erik," Anne whispered to herself. "Shit."

She was still staring out the window five minutes later, watching the waves lap gently at the rocks of the cove, when her cell phone vibrated to life on her kitchen table, playing a salsa style ringtone.

"Hey, Celeste," she said.

"Hey girl, how's life on the island?" Celeste shouted.

"Not bad," Anne replied, "the leeches have returned."

The other residents of Pine Island had more polite terms to make fun of the throngs of people that provided their livelihoods each summer, but Anne called them leeches because that's what they were: little parasitic worms that sucked the lifeblood out of the island and then slithered back home.

"How's your garden doing?" Celeste asked.

"Alright," Anne said.

"A one-word answer, about your garden? What's up, lady?"

"How long has it been since Steven and I broke up?" Anne asked.

"You broke up with him right before you moved to the island, so it's been, like, two years," Celeste replied. "Why? What's wrong? Is he there?"

"No," Anne said. "Last I heard, he was still in New York setting the financial world on fire."

"Is that a hint of jealousy I hear?" Celeste asked. "You know, you're the one that decided to cash out and run away from it all. I'm sure there are a dozen firms that would snap you up in a heartbeat."

"It's not that," Anne replied, "I'm loving this independence and I needed a break. You were there, you know my whole life was out of control. No, I'm just trying to remember *how long it's been*."

"How long it's been since...oh, sweetie," Celeste said sympathetically, "are you telling me you haven't been with anyone since Steven? What about that guy we met at the bar on New Year's Eve, or the college professor, what was his name?"

"I don't remember, but no, nothing like that happened with either of them," Anne said, looking out the kitchen window at the footbridge. "I didn't realize it had been that long."

"Leave it to me," Celeste said. "When I'm there for the 4th, we'll find you a tanned, young stud with something to prove. He'll fuck you like thunder for three-and-a-half minutes and swear you were the best he's ever had. Trust me, I've got this."

"Stop!" Anne laughed.

"I'm serious," Celeste laughed back. "He'll actually make your thighs tremble, just like in one of those juicy novels you like to read."

"When did this happen to me?" Anne groaned. "Since when do I need a man to feel complete?"

"Oh, right, I forgot you're Jane of the Jungle now," Celeste scoffed. "All you need is a good book and a steady supply of rechargeable batteries for that big black –"

"Enough!" Anne shouted.

"Whatever," Celeste chirped. "You brought it up."

"I should know better than to open that door for you," said Anne, "but it's not just about sex. Some guy just pulled into the inlet in his boat and I completely froze up like a teenager. It's like I've completely forgotten how to talk to people."

"Hmm," Celeste responded, "did you use the shotgun?"

"No," Anne giggled, "I let him use the bathroom."

"What's wrong with that?" Celeste started shouting again. "I love you, girl, but you need to admit that you had some sort of breakdown out here in New York. When you weren't talking about missing the island, you were raging against everyone and everything. You remember that guy in the suit? It's a miracle you didn't get charged for that."

How could Anne forget? She and Celeste were grabbing a hot dog at a stand on the street when a hipster in a tight blue suit and tan shoes told his buddies to check out her '*bangin tits.*' Anne punched him so hard in the gut that he doubled over, then added insult to injury by shoving him onto the pavement. His friends started to protest, but when they saw the wild look on Anne's face and the pepper spray in Celeste's hand, they just helped their friend to his feet and scurried away.

"He had it coming," Anne said.

"That's not the point," Celeste replied. "Maybe this isn't just a timeout. Maybe you're working on a whole new you? Personally, I'd rather have you tongue tied than assaulting every stranger that ignores your sign."

"Hmmph," Anne grumbled.

Celeste had a knack for cutting to the heart of Anne's issues, but even her best friend didn't know how bad things really were when Anne was crashing and burning in New York; how Anne played the day's conversations over and over in her head to the point that she couldn't get to sleep; how she would wake up in a panic, cringing about something she said in a meeting weeks ago; how even her past victories felt like defeats inside her twisted web of hindsight. Things were better on the island, but Anne didn't know if she'd ever be truly comfortable around other people again.

"Oh, before I forget," Celeste said excitedly, "did you see that they released another season of *Zombie Manifesto* yesterday? How far did you get?"

"I only got through the first one," Anne lied.

She'd managed to experience six seasons of horror porn without ever watching a single episode. All it took was the mere pretense of reality, and Celeste would be off to the races. Today was no different. She immediately jumped into a diatribe about the futility of the battle for control of post-apocalyptic Chicago, how the three factions needed to get a clue and start combining forces against Arch-Priestess Zoe, instead of stupidly fighting each other. From both a tactical and a reproductive standpoint, control of the sewers was key.

Anne sighed.

Deep down, all she really wanted was another long, lonely summer.

***

Dylan sat on the picnic bench, his thumb sliding slowly back and forth across the serrated blade of his wine key. He watched the ferry from Pine Island steam across the sparkling waters of Lake Huron and tried to ignore the pain in his legs. It was still early in the summer, but the tourist season was in full swing. The ferries were running more frequently now, bringing families and their vehicles back and forth to Eagleton. As he contemplated his disaster of a life, the only thing keeping him grounded in the here and now was the dull ache that began in his heels and ran up into his knees. It was the kind of pain he had experienced every day since he started waiting tables, the kind of pain Kyle referred to as '*building character*.'

Fuck character.

What Dylan needed was a million bucks that someone else forgot, or maybe a time machine.

He needed his wife.

Dylan had never been so low, and suicide was a constant companion, always lurking on the fringes of his mind. It wasn't that he wanted to die, he just couldn't remember how to live. He took a sip of whiskey from his flask and wondered if he could join Mary on the other side. If he took his own life – ended it like she had – would she be there waiting for him? Would she welcome him with open arms to ferry him to the world beyond?

With a sigh, he repositioned his grip, moved the wine key to his throat and felt the tip of the blade grab hold of its mark. He closed his eyes and pictured the flesh opening, the warm red flow of his shattered hopes and dreams splashing onto the ground.

"Hey! Let's go, Dylan, your single is waiting and I'm tired of covering for you!" A young waiter shouted out a screen door and trotted away without waiting for a reply.

Fucking Jimmy.

Dylan hated that kid.

His latest vision for a glorious end to a miserable year would have to wait. He took another shot of whiskey from his flask, concealed it in the pocket behind his server's apron, and walked through the back door. It was well past nine o'clock on a Wednesday, but the heat and raw energy still blasted him in the face. The kitchen was alive with the clanging of metal spatulas, pans dancing across cast iron, the earthy smell of sautéed mushrooms, and of course the barking of Kyle, chef and master of this domain. At six foot five and two-hundred-forty pounds, Kyle was hard to miss anywhere, but in the kitchen – his kitchen – he had a commanding presence.

"Move it buddy, and remember to push the oysters," Kyle said, quickly moving on to his next task. "Jimmy! You're up! Get this out of my face, kid!"

Jimmy quickly obliged, positioning a crisp linen towel over his forearm, putting the prime rib and crab-stuffed filet of grouper on a serving tray and striding out of the kitchen.

Dylan pushed his way through the double swinging doors and out into the main dining room. The dim lighting of the restaurant was a stark contrast to the kitchen. *The Traveler's Hearth* was a nice place, a step above most generic chain restaurants, with gourmet American food that was modestly priced and served in a unique atmosphere. The décor was eclectic to say the least. Greek busts mingled with modern sculptures, magnificent faux ferns, black tables and chairs with straight lines, and dazzling white linens. The focal point of the entire dining area was a magnificent fieldstone hearth with a wood burning fireplace. It was Dylan's favorite part of the restaurant, and he often caught himself staring into the flames while customers repeated their orders through his daydreaming.

Dylan spotted his single and walked over. With his hair deliberately mussed and his half-shaven face, the man looked like he could be on a highway billboard in his underwear, selling – well – *anything.* Dylan didn't know why he was eating alone, but he didn't care. He just wanted the night to be over.

"Hello, Dylan, it's nice to finally see you," the man said, preempting Dylan's stale, generic greeting. "I'd like a dozen of the oysters," the man continued without looking up. "James tells me they're outstanding right now and should pair nicely with the cabernet he selected for me."

"Uh, yes," Dylan said, "I would definitely agree. I was able to sample a few myself earlier today and they are quite good. The best oysters you'll find a thousand miles from the ocean, I can tell you that much." Dylan grinned.

"To start, I'll go with your house salad," the man said, ignoring Dylan's half-hearted attempt to be friendly. "Are the greens local?"

"Yes. Reynold's Farm, just a few miles down the—"

"Wonderful," he interrupted, closing the menu. He handed it to Dylan and turned his attention to a sci-fi novel that he had on his lap.

No wonder this guy is alone, Dylan thought.

Dylan went through the motions, taking care of his final customer of the night, but his mind was on the other side of town, nestled into the cool patch of earth where Mary waited for him. As was usually the case, the final customer of the night ordered dessert *and* a cup of coffee. When he was finally able to finish clearing the table, Dylan picked up the book that contained the bill.

"It's been a pleasure taking care of you tonight," Dylan said blankly. Noticing a few bills protruding from the end of the book, he added, "I'll be right back with your change."

"I won't be needing any change," the man said, getting up from his chair and walking away.

Prick, Dylan thought.

He noticed the man had forgotten his novel and he picked it up without hesitation. He went back to the server's station, threw the book into the trash, and started to reconcile the bill. The man had counted out exact change, but left Dylan a single penny for his efforts.

As Abe Lincoln's face mocked him, Dylan's anger boiled over.

"Hey, Jimmy!" He shouted.

Dylan strode deliberately into the kitchen, where he found the source of his frustration chatting up one of the female line cooks. "What the fuck, Jimmy?" He slammed down the faux-leather book in frustration. "Why didn't you just take that table? The guy stiffed me!"

"Don't blame me. I would have taken the table, but Kyle said it was yours," Jimmy said, turning his attention back to his female friend.

"Don't give me that shit," Dylan shouted. He took a step towards Jimmy, his face flush with anger. "You just let him sit there? Didn't bring him his drink or anything?"

Slam! The sound of a twelve-inch sauté pan hitting the stainless countertop stopped Dylan in his tracks. Everyone in the kitchen stopped moving and looked at Kyle.

"Knock it off!" He roared.

Jimmy stared at Kyle like a puppy who just got caught shitting on the rug. "Jimmy, you got the coolers tonight. Make sure they're prepped for tomorrow. Move it."

Jimmy scurried away without a word.

"Dylan, outside." Kyle pointed to the screen door with his skillet. "Now."

When they got outside, Kyle grabbed Dylan by the collar.

"You need to get your shit together, my friend," he said, tightening his grip for emphasis. "Everybody knows what happened, Dylan, even the new kids like Jimmy, but I can't keep playing referee to your frustration. You can't keep taking it out on everyone else!"

Dylan pried at his friend's hand, and Kyle released his grip with a shove.

"Here," he said, putting some money into Dylan's hand. "You're off the next couple of days. That should cover your tips."

Dylan looked down at the money in his hand. "Come on –"

"I'm serious," Kyle interrupted, "you need a break, and quite frankly, we all need a break from you. You think I can't smell your breath, shithead?"

The heat of Dylan's anger was replaced by the warmth of his embarrassment.

"I'm sorry," he managed.

"Yeah, we'll see how sorry you are when you start working in my kitchen," Kyle said, "and one more thing – if you come within a mile of the restaurant before you get properly laid, I'm cracking your skull."

He pointed the sauté pan at Dylan's face and then went back into the kitchen.

"Let's go, folks," Kyle growled as the screen door creaked open. "Shut it down, clean it up and put it away."

Dylan looked at the money in his hand, ashamed and exhausted. From inside, he heard Kyle and the line cooks start trading dirty jokes to make the clean-up go faster, a sexually explicit ballet of sophomoric brinksmanship.

Dylan took a long pull from his flask and started to walk home.

***

Erik removed his camera from its watertight housing and retrieved the data card. He smiled as the images of his dive unfolded on his computer screen. He scribbled a few notes and then paused the video as the strange markings from the wall came into view. He took a picture of the screen with his phone, then punched in a number from memory.

"Hey buddy, what do you need?"

Frank Stone only got calls from Erik when he needed something. As a state historian he didn't make a lot of money, and Erik didn't have a lot of knowledge. It was a perfect match.

"I've got an image I need help with," Erik said. "I need to know what it is."

"The usual?" Frank asked.

If this was as big as Erik suspected, that would be a bargain.

"Sure," Erik replied.

He pushed send on his cell phone and waited for Frank to receive it.

"How deep were you? Where was this?" Frank's hurried tone confirmed Erik's suspicions.

"Pine Island, right in my backyard," Erik replied. "Honestly, I was just scrounging around looking for lost tackle and other trash to sell when I found the cave."

"Well, we have to have a serious conversation, Erik," Frank said.

"Why is that?" Erik smiled.

"Did you find any artifacts?" Frank asked.

That question was a good sign.

"Nope," Erik lied.

"Look, this is huge. This is the finest example of stone age markings I've ever seen around here. How deep were you?"

"About fifty feet," he replied.

"If you shot this image over 40 feet deep these markings haven't seen the light of day for about 6,000 years." Frank paused. "Are you messing around, Erik?"

"No, I swear to you, this is exactly what I found."

"Deal's off, then. The usual arrangement doesn't apply here," Frank continued. "You gotta do this legit. I'm telling you, this is big."

Erik's smile relaxed slightly. It was private property.

"Alright," Erik said.

"Like I said," Frank replied. "When people around here see this, there's going to be a feeding frenzy. Dr. Parsons is gonna flip."

"I'll be in touch," Erik said.

"You got it – oh, and Erik?" Frank paused. "Congratulations."

Erik smiled and hung up the phone.

The fact that this was on private land complicated things, but if the way Anne had stared at him was any indication, it wouldn't be hard to get her to cooperate.

CHAPTER THREE

Dylan sat in his recliner and stared quietly out the window of his apartment at the creeping darkness of dusk. Since he didn't have to work, he had spent most of the day sleeping and drinking. His apartment was basic. A small, one-bedroom flat was all he needed. There was no way he could keep living in the house after Mary died, but he couldn't find anyone that didn't know what had happened. Dylan had walked away from his career, and when no buyers surfaced, it was just as easy to walk away from his mortgage. Given that his credit was shit, he only got this place on the understanding that he would pay his rent in bi-weekly cash installments.

"I have a heart," his landlord had said, "but I don't do charity."

So far, Dylan hadn't missed a payment.

A streetlamp flicked on outside, establishing a pale-yellow foothold on the sidewalk across the street. Dylan poured another splash of whiskey into the rocks glass on the end table. He took a sip and savored the biting sweetness before taking its warmth into his throat. He had started drinking while Mary was still alive, self-medicating to cope with the constant stress of her mental illness. Since she died, alcohol was the only consistent thing in his life, and it covered him like a shroud.

He glanced at his cell phone and wondered if he should call Jillian back. She had called earlier in the day, but she didn't leave a message. She never did. A 'missed call' tag was all Dylan needed to know that sex was only a phone call away. Part of him wanted to call – he didn't understand how his penis could be so cold-hearted – but ever since Mary started to appear in the cemetery, the thought of being with another woman felt like cheating.

With a sigh and a final glance out the window, Dylan pushed a few buttons on his phone and waited while it rang on the other end.

"Hey, I'm starting to think that you don't like me." Jillian answered, pretending to sound pouty.

"Yeah, time got away from me today."

"Kyle told me you were drinking at the cemetery again last night," Jillian said. "I'm worried about you, Dylan. We all are."

"I'm fine. I'm just working through this in my own way." The sudden silence of their conversation confirmed what Dylan was feeling. He shouldn't have called.

"Well," Jillian's tone brightened, "the kids are with their dad tonight. Why don't I come by and try to help you forget about the world for a few hours?"

"I can't, Jillian," was all Dylan could manage.

"Oh, stop," she replied, "you can drink with me instead of by yourself, alright? Sometimes it's nice to have a friend to talk to."

Jillian clearly needed something tonight, but his heart longed for Mary. He shot down the rest of the whiskey in his glass, then replied, "Alright."

Dylan got up from the recliner and stared at the clutter of his unwanted bachelorhood. He had just enough time to get the dishes into the sink, and his dirty clothes into the hamper before three gentle knocks announced Jillian's arrival. He forced a half smile before he opened the door and her mischievous brown eyes caught his. Her shirt was unbuttoned practically to her navel, and it looked like she'd shed weight from her already spare frame since the last time he saw her.

"I brought Moscato," she said, shaking the brown paper bag in her left hand and taking a hit from the bottle already open in her right. Dylan got a couple of glasses and opened the wine while Jillian settled into the couch. Dylan couldn't help but admire the shape of her hips and the sweet, vanilla scent of her perfume. He walked over to the couch and gave her a glass he had filled nearly to the top.

"Oh, right," she said and gulped down what was left in the other bottle before taking the glass from Dylan's outstretched hand. "Cheers," she said and took a sip.

"How do you do it?" Dylan asked, looking at Jillian's smiling face.

She glanced down at her open blouse, grinned and said, "Hours at the gym. I watch what I eat, and I have a standing appointment at the salon. And I'm a bit of a label whore," she added with a wink, "but that's what my alimony payments are for."

"No, not that." Dylan grinned. "How do you go on without him? Don't you have any feelings left? You just seem so put together — slightly intoxicated, but confident."

"I'm telling you, Dylan, my divorce was a blessing."

"Oh, come on," Dylan said incredulously, "wasn't there any love between you?"

"We were madly in love at one point." Jillian's face relaxed slightly. "Our days were filled with each other, you know? It was the kind of love where you can't concentrate on anything at work, and you find yourself standing in the laundry room staring out the window daydreaming."

"So, what happened?"

"I don't know," she replied, "we just grew apart. Between the kids, our careers, and the pace of life, we just didn't have any time for each other. It was like we were roommates. We shared a house and loved our kids, but when it all boiled down, we were just paying bills and going through the motions."

"That all seems pretty typical," Dylan said. "No endless fighting, no intolerable in-laws, no dishes hurled across the kitchen in fits of rage?"

"No," Jillian said. "We just stopped caring." She looked genuinely sad. "You want to know how it ended? The actual, final moment when I knew it was over?"

"Go on," Dylan said.

"I'd had a terrible day at work. He came home, and I was trying to open up to him," Jillian said. "He sat down on the couch and he just turned on the TV – he didn't even look at me or acknowledge what I said – and then he asked if I would get him a beer."

"Ouch," Dylan said. "Would you like a beer, instead? I think I have one."

"Fuck off."

"No, sorry," he said, "I see what you mean. Maybe your divorce was a blessing."

"So, is that how it was with you and Mary?" Jillian asked. "Arguing? Shattered dishes?"

"Toward the end, yeah," he replied, "but things didn't get like that until her mental illness really took hold. It was like watching a train wreck in slow motion. I watched her change, little by little, day after day, until she was practically a stranger."

"So, how did you manage?"

"I learned how to duck," Dylan said and smiled. "We got her into therapy, I found support groups, meds, group therapy for us, meds for me, more meds for her." He took a long sip of his wine. "And I learned to cope."

"Yeah," she said, "your coping skills are legendary."

"Pot to kettle," Dylan said and drained his glass.

"So, tell me about the good times," Jillian said.

"Our love was effortless," Dylan replied. "It wasn't something we had to work on or make time for. I know it sounds silly, but it was like we completed each other. Do you believe in soulmates?"

"Not so much," Jillian replied and downed the rest of the wine in her glass. She tossed her hair with one hand and settled back into the couch, her breasts begging to be freed from the prison of her black lace bra. "I'm more into fuck buddies, right now."

"Look, Jillian, I –"

"Relax, Dylan," she said, reading his face, "we don't have to do anything you're not up for. Sometimes it's just nice to have a warm body to lay with."

She stood up, wobbled, and leaned over until her rosy cheeks were inches from Dylan's face.

"Truth be told," she said, "I just didn't want to be alone tonight."

She tugged gently at Dylan's hand, grabbed the other bottle of wine and took another drink. She raised her eyebrows, licked her lips seductively then unbuttoned the last few buttons of her blouse as she shuffled backwards into the kitchen.

"We're gonna hit it old school, Mr. Sad Pants," she said and queued up *All the Small Things* by blink-182 on her phone. She thumped two shot glasses on the kitchen table. "Time to show me what you're made of," she said, filling each shot glass with whiskey and sitting down.

Dylan sat at the opposite side of the table and grabbed the shot glass in front of him. He downed it in a single gulp without flinching. Jillian shot her whiskey and pounded the table with her fist before chasing it down with a hit from the wine bottle.

"Ouch!" she groaned, filling both glasses again, and pushing them in front of Dylan.

He swallowed them one after the other while she clapped and hollered approval. Dylan filled the shot glasses again, but Jillian gave him a playful frown.

"You win," she said, getting up from the table. She threw her shirt at his face, slipped out of her pants and started to dance while she lip-synced to the tune pounding away on the kitchen table.

Say it ain't so

I will not go

Turn the lights off

Carry me home

"Na-na, na-na, na-na, na-na, na-na!" Jillian shouted at the ceiling. "Get up and dance with me, you loser! Oh, wait." She fumbled with her phone, trying to keep her balance. "Yeah, that's what I need," she said as *Fat Lip* by Sum 41 started up.

As the guitars began to hammer away, she threw her arms in the air and shook her head from side to side, jumping up and down in rhythm.

I will never fall in line

Become another victim of your conformity

And back down!

When the chorus finished and the guitars pulsed into the bridge, she slowed down, swaying her hips from side to side and looking at Dylan over her shoulder.

Dylan had never liked to dance but watching wasn't so bad.

"So, what exactly do they mean by *kufuffin*?" he asked, a desperate attempt to ignore the black lace hip-huggers in front of his face. "That lyric has always confused me."

"Follow me, and I'll show you," Jillian replied and giggled her way into the bedroom.

Dylan followed and sat down on the edge of the bed where Jillian had face-planted.

"See? It's not so bad," she said playfully. "Life goes on, Dyly-dyly. Oh, I know! Let's binge something on Netflix!"

"Sorry, I don't have wi-fi, or unlimited data," he said, "or Netflix."

"You need to ask Kyle for a raise," she said sleepily.

Dylan brushed her hair back behind her ear and massaged her temple. When she started to snore, he grabbed his pillow and a spare blanket, then headed to the couch.

***

The smell of death and fear surrounded Dylan in the darkness, but he wasn't afraid. In the distance, drums pounded frantically, their rhythm a unified cadence. His heart pounded and his chest heaved in anticipation.

Dylan looked at the blunt weapon in his hand, its raw power mingling with the adrenaline that coursed through his body. He felt the energy flow through him, building like a storm with the beating drums, until he couldn't contain it. He let out a scream, releasing the energy from the depths of his soul and into the darkness.

Around him, other screams answered his call, until his head was filled only with their echoes and the beating of the drums. Their shouts began to grunt in unison with the drums, and Dylan drew strength from the darkness around him. His body tensed and his grip tightened around the bloody instrument he clutched in his hand.

Letting out another cry, he charged ahead into the mist...

Dylan. Wake up.

The sound of Mary's voice brought Dylan awake with a start. He sat up on the couch, his heart still pounding from the dream. He strained against the darkness, listening for Mary's voice, but there was nothing.

Dylan checked the bedroom and watched Jillian's slumbered breathing for a few moments before heading to the kitchen. He stood over the kitchen sink and let the cool water run over his head. His heartbeat began to return to normal, and the heat ran out of his limbs, rinsing away with the water down the drain. Tipping his head to the side, he took a long drink, and dried off his hair and face with the towel hanging from the stove.

When he turned to go back to the couch, he stopped in his tracks. He stood paralyzed, unable to breathe, and looked into the eyes of his dead wife. She smiled warmly from across the kitchen table, her face radiant and inviting. Dylan felt his heart skip a beat. He had never seen Mary outside of the cemetery.

"Mary," Dylan gasped and took a tentative step forward. "Is it really you?"

She closed the distance between them.

"It's me," she whispered softly.

Dylan held her in his arms, the warmth of her breath on his ear betraying reality.

"My God, Mary," Dylan choked out the words, tears filling his eyes. "What's going on? How is this possible?"

Mary gently broke off their embrace and looked into his eyes.

"I'm here to help you, Dylan. Do what she says, you have to read it."

"Do as who says? Read what?" Dylan pleaded. "What are you talking about, Mary? Please, tell me what's going on!"

Mary was about to say something, when her head snapped back, and shook violently from side to side. The warmth and love were replaced by the cold accusing eyes, disheveled hair and bruised neck that haunted him. The air in Dylan's kitchen came alive with desperate, whispered voices that circled around his head and left an icy trail across the back of his neck. With a smile that curled into a sneer, Mary looked directly into Dylan's eyes, then looked over his shoulder towards the bedroom where Jillian was sleeping.

"Was it worth it, Dylan?" Mary's eyes narrowed. "Throwing away everything we have to fuck some whore?" She grabbed him by the neck with one hand, her vacant, accusing eyes inches from his. "I'm right here, Dyly-dyly," she said mockingly "come fuck me!"

The stench from her mouth turned Dylan's stomach. It was like roadkill, mixed with steaming compost and rancid milk. His lungs burned, his vision blurred, and he gasped for air as she laughed and tightened her grip around his throat.

Then suddenly she disappeared, blinking out like a light, leaving Dylan alone and confused. He took in a deep breath and coughed, then slumped into a chair at the kitchen table. Instinctively, he reached for the bottle of whiskey. He filled a glass half full, quickly shot it down and closed his eyes.

Dylan sat in his kitchen and considered that he might be losing his grip on reality. He had never seen Mary outside the cemetery, and despite the violence of the encounter, he was consumed by thoughts of his wife. She called to him from across town, and he had to see her again, to continue their conversation.

He heard Jillian stirring in the bedroom, and she walked out a few seconds later, wrapped in Dylan's bedsheet. She opened her mouth to say something, but bolted to the bathroom instead, and emptied her stomach. When she finished gagging, she flushed the toilet, washed her face and walked back into the kitchen.

She cleared her throat, tossed her hair back over her shoulder and smiled. She looked like a disco ball at dawn, captivating and radiant, but reeking of vomit and regret from the night before.

She noticed the bottle of whiskey and the glass on the kitchen table.

"Still going?" She asked in a gravelly voice. "By yourself?"

"Just a quick shot to clear my head," Dylan brushed her off.

"Don't you ever get hungover?"

"Only when I stop," Dylan replied and poured another shot.

"Well," she padded across the floor, leaving the sheet in a trail behind her. When she got to the bedroom, she stopped and turned around, leaning against the door so Dylan could fully appreciate her half-naked form. "You know where to find me if you change your mind."

She barely got the words out before scurrying back to the bathroom and retching again.

Dylan got her a glass of water and helped her back into bed.

"I'm sorry," she said, "I don't usually drink so much."

"No need to apologize," Dylan said. "I enjoyed the uh...show, last night."

Jillian gave him the middle finger.

"Get some rest," Dylan said. "I'm going to take a walk, but I'll make you some breakfast later this morning, okay?"

Jillian put a hand over her mouth and groaned.

"Ugh, don't talk about food."

As soon as she started to snore, he grabbed his keys and slipped quietly out the door.

***

It was still dark when Dylan reached the cemetery. Like he had a hundred times before, he vaulted the fence and started up the path toward the Union soldier. The wind had shifted, blowing from the north, across the cold, open expanse of Lake Huron before making landfall. There was a chill in the air, and the cemetery was blanketed with a gray mist.

As he walked past the soldier, movement off to his left caught his eye. He stopped when a shadow darted across the grass and disappeared behind a shrub.

"Hello? Is someone there?"

Off to his right, another small form shot out, ran a zig-zag path between the rows of headstones, then disappeared behind a pine tree. Dylan took a few tentative steps down the path.

"Hello?"

Dylan held his breath as a little girl came out from behind the tree and into the moonlight. She wore a white, knee-length gown with poufy arms that buttoned into a high, ruffled collar around her neck. Her clothes were long out of fashion, right down to the dark stockings and simple leather shoes that laced up past her ankle. Her light brown hair was tied up in a black bow, with curls dancing down onto her shoulders.

"You're the one that keeps coming to visit, aren't you?"

Despite his many conversations with Mary, Dylan didn't know what to say. She was the only dead person he had ever talked to, and somehow, he couldn't find the words.

"No!" whispered another young voice from the shadows.

A slightly older girl, dressed almost identically to the one in front of him, came out from behind the tree. She hurried over to the other girl and tugged at her arm.

"Remember what Mother said!" she whispered.

"Hush, Constance! You wouldn't be here if you didn't want to talk to him, too." She turned to Dylan. "Mother says we aren't supposed to speak to you."

"Oh," Dylan managed.

"Do you have the light?" the younger girl asked, a curious look on her face. "Lots of people come to visit us, especially when we get a new neighbor. I pick flowers for them, I say hello to them, sometimes I even throw stones at them to get their attention. But they never see me." She took a few steps forward. "But you can see me. Why?"

"I – I honestly don't know," Dylan felt a cool sweat begin on his forehead. "Why does your mother say you shouldn't talk to me?"

"Margaret, no!" Constance rushed over to the bookend tombstone and looked nervously at her mother's grave.

Ignoring her sister, Margaret walked over to Dylan until she was close enough to touch him. "Mother says that you're special."

"Special?" Dylan asked.

"She's right, you know," said Margaret, "You're very bright. I can see it every time you come to visit. Right here," she arched up on the toes of her leather shoes, stretched out her index finger and touched Dylan on the chest, just over his heart.

"Margaret!" Constance had reached her limit. "We have to go!" She shouted and grabbed her sister's hand. Margaret smiled and ran away with her sister, their ponytails bobbing along behind them. Dylan watched as their forms went from darkness to shadow and then disappeared into the night.

The cemetery was suddenly turned upside down, and it took Dylan a few minutes to gather his wits. Coming here had always been about Mary, and he had never been bothered by the totality of death that surrounded him. The thought of others coming out for a chat made Dylan shiver. When he was sure the little girls were gone, he continued down the path, relieved when the willow tree and Mary's headstone came into view. He sat down, settled into his favorite spot among the roots, and took a deep breath.

"I need to talk to you, Mary," he whispered. "Please, talk to me."

"Mary...Mary..."

The mocking, husky tone of Mary's voice brought Dylan spinning to his feet, and he instinctively took a couple steps backward. The form on the other side of the tree stood still, but even through the limbs of the willow, Dylan could make out the battered features of his dead wife's face.

"What's the matter, Dylan?" she asked sarcastically, hands on her hips. "Not who you were hoping for?" She took a step forward, but he countered her movement, stepping to the left to keep the base of the tree between them. Mary leapt into the tree in a single, swift motion, and Dylan fell backward over the roots in surprise. Before he could get up, she scurried out onto a branch on all fours until she was directly above him.

"You should be more careful, Dylan." Mary said, looking down at him from her perch. "When you come calling, others can hear you."

His judgment was clouded by whiskey, and in spite of their rough encounter in his kitchen, Dylan still had a single thought on his mind.

"I want to talk to my wife," Dylan said, standing up. "Where is she?"

Mary sat on the branch, swayed from side to side and chuckled.

"I said, where's my wife you fucking—"

"Temper, temper, darling," she said, jumping to the ground before he could finish his thought. "I'm right here. Don't you recognize me in my favorite outfit?" She spun around with a flourish, as if twirling a dress, but she was wearing blue jeans and a grey cotton sweatshirt. "Pity it got all bloody that day you were off arguing in court."

Dylan was running out of patience and he repeated his demand through clenched teeth.

"Where is she?"

In an instant, his dead wife's face went from amused to angry. She spanned the short distance between them, grabbed Dylan by the shoulders and let out a shrill scream. A sharp pain started in the center of his chest, then turned to raw heat as the air was sucked out of his lungs. The shriek grew louder until there was nothing but a dull roar ringing in his ears. Her iron grip twisted like a vise, and she lifted Dylan into the air, shaking him like a ragdoll. As he struggled to breathe, stars appeared on the edge of his vision, and he felt his bladder empty into his jeans and run down his leg.

As Dylan's world faded to black, a woman appeared under the willow behind Mary. Even in the half-light of dawn, Dylan could see her crimson hair glowing against her black dress. Mary dropped Dylan to the ground, then spun around to face her.

"He belongs to me," Mary said, pacing back and forth in front of Dylan.

"He carries the light," the woman said and took a step forward.

"As do you," said Mary through clenched teeth. "I was given this place, to hunt his kind. To hunt *your* kind."

"It's one thing to prey upon those that lack knowledge of their gift," the woman said, "but have you ever fed from one who knows?"

"I've watched many just like you," Mary snickered, "gasping for air, trying to scream, as they wasted away to nothing in my hands."

"Hunting in packs during the schism, perhaps," the woman said and took a step forward, "but one-on-one? Alone?"

The woman closed her eyes and Dylan felt a thump in his chest. She raised her hands, her red hair billowing around her head, and a hum started in Dylan's ears. It changed pitch, as if searching for the right frequency, and then locked into a rhythm.

Mary grabbed her ears in pain and shrieked. She looked at Dylan, hissed at the woman in disgust, and then disappeared into the darkness.

The woman lowered her arms and the hum faded away. Her hair gradually relaxed and braided itself neatly back into place.

"My name is Abigail," the woman said. "You've met my girls, I believe?"

Constance and Margaret appeared from behind the tree and stood next to their mother.

"I...I don't..." Dylan stuttered.

"I'd love to wait for you to finish that thought, Dylan, but I really must insist we find a safer place to talk."

Abigail held out her hand and helped Dylan to his feet.

"How much do you know about your ancestors?"

CHAPTER FOUR

Anne sat on one of the stones at the top of the hill and rested. The circuit around her grandfather's island was about a quarter-mile, but the incline of the hill made it feel considerably farther, and Anne needed to catch her breath. While she sat sweating and admiring the morning sun, a familiar boat came into view.

"Shit!" Anne shouted to herself.

She started down the path that ended at the footbridge, getting there just in time to see Erik Larson come around the rocks. He smiled and waved as Anne emerged from the trees.

"Remember me?" Erik shouted. "It's Anne, right?"

He threw a line onto the footbridge and pulled it taunt around one of the pilings.

"Yeah," Anne replied. She didn't see any dive gear. "You decided to stay in your boat this time?"

"Right," Erik said, "that's kind of why I'm here. I really should have asked for your permission before I started diving around here, and I wanted to apologize. I wondered if you were up for a picnic lunch?"

Anne was wearing a pair of black spandex running shorts and a white sports bra that left very little to the imagination. Erik's eyes looked her up and down while he waited for a response, pausing at her hips and again at her chest.

He didn't even try to pretend like he wasn't looking.

"I'm not exactly dressed for a picnic," Anne said, adjusting her bra and then crossing her arms. "What did you have in mind?"

"I stopped by Haggerty's and got some of their smoked whitefish," Erik said. "I've got some gouda cheese and a bottle of late harvest Riesling from the winery across the bay in the cooler." He smiled big – obviously proud of himself – before adding, "Want to hop into my boat and we'll head over to Grant Park?"

Anne got the feeling Erik Larson had done this before.

"How about my front porch?" Anne smiled back. "But I need to change first."

"Take your time." Erik kicked up his feet on the console and turned on his radio. The sound of drums, power chords and someone screaming angry lyrics echoed up the path and into the trees. "See you in a few!"

Anne returned wearing much more modest attire, but she was still conflicted about how to deal with Erik. It was so much easier to be alone, after all. She could fake a stomachache, pretend to throw up in the bushes next to the porch and then safely bury herself under the blankets on the couch. Then again, maybe Celeste was right? Maybe she needed a meaningless fling to get this bad juju out of her system. There was a part of her that wanted to tie Erik up on the footbridge, right next to the 'no trespassing' sign, rip his clothes off with her bare hands, and then ravage his tight, water-logged little scuba body, until all 18 months of her self-imposed nunnery had been thoroughly dealt with.

"I have to admit this isn't the type of thing I usually do," Anne sat down on her front porch steps and tried to act casual.

"Oh, come on," Erik replied, "a pretty girl like you. You must have all the eligible guys on the island swimming up to your door." He handed her a red plastic cup, unscrewed the top of the wine bottle and filled her glass halfway.

Anne took a small sip, using the wine as an excuse to not make eye contact. Her grandfather had taught her to use all her senses to savor wine. She closed her eyes, breathing in through her nose and chewing the liquid before she swallowed. It was sweet, light and refreshing. The grapes took shape in her mind. Anne imagined the earth across the bay where the grapes had been harvested, nourishing them long into the fall until their sweetness was almost bursting from their flesh.

"Not bad, eh?" Erik said matter-of-factly.

Anne gave him a sideways glance.

"Late harvest has always been their best effort," she said. "They really know what they're doing."

"Yeah." Erik shifted uncomfortably. "Look, Anne, I have something I need to ask you." He looked directly into her eyes. His gaze was so intense that, for a moment, she forgot to breathe, and she felt a small, involuntary spasm tickle the inside of her thigh.

"I found something on your island," Erik said, "well, under your island. I'm not sure what it is yet, but I have a friend in the state archeology office who thinks it's important."

Erik paused, letting his words sink in.

"I don't understand," Anne replied, genuinely confused, then looked down at her glass to escape the intensity of his gaze. "What did you find?"

"It's some sort of cave," Erik said. "There's etchings on the walls and it looks like it was used for something thousands of years ago."

"Did you say thousands? How is that even possible?"

"Yeah, that's what we think. Back when the glaciers were receding, the lake levels were lower, and the cave would have been on dry land. But to be sure..." Erik paused. "To be sure, we have to excavate. It looks like the best way to do that is to dig down from the surface and to do some more intensive work underwater. I think the rocks above the cave have something to do with the markings I saw on the wall, but I can't be sure unless we do some excavation on the surface."

"We? Who is we?" Anne asked. "And how do you know about the rocks on my hill?"

"Like I said, I've been in touch with the office of the state archaeologist, Jim Parsons," Erik said. "He's really excited about this. He told me he's never seen anything like it around here. We're all going to be famous!"

Erik was visibly excited, smiling ear to ear. He drained his glass in a single gulp and filled it again. The wine in Anne's mouth went sour. The island was a special place for Anne, a spiritual place where she connected with higher energies, but her craft was private. There was no way she was going to share that with anyone, and she certainly didn't want to be famous.

"I need your permission, Anne. I can file the paperwork and take care of everything, but I need your permission because it's your property."

Erik waited.

As it turned out, isolation wasn't Anne's only option today. Somehow, she knew that Erik Larson was too good to be true, and she felt the anger creep down her arm and into her hand. Without hesitating, she threw what was left of her wine directly into his face. Erik grabbed his eyes and blinked at her in stinging disbelief.

"Goodbye, Mr. Larson," Anne said and stood up.

"Wait!" Erik stood up. "Wait, let me explain."

"No," Anne walked inside and latched the screen door. "The answer is no. And if I ever see you by my grandfather's island again, I'm calling the police."

Anne shut the front door and shoved home the deadbolt.

Erik pounded on the door.

"Anne, come on," he shouted, "let me explain!"

Anne opened the front door and let it slam into the other side of the door frame for dramatic effect. Erik didn't know what was more terrifying: the look of pure hatred on her face, or the shotgun resting on her hip.

"No, Erik," Anne said with mock sweetness. "Get your shit off my porch, and go, the fuck, away."

Erik held up his hands and obediently complied. He gathered up the picnic, boarded his boat, and made haste for the safety of the open waters of Lake Huron. Even though she was armed, Erik still believed in his heart of hearts that he could make her come around. She wasn't the first woman – or jealous significant other – that had confronted him with a deadly weapon.

He simply didn't have the patience.

As he motored ahead, hugging the coast and heading back home, he took out his phone and opened his YouTube account. He expected the word Stonehenge to generate tons of hits, so he posted the video of the cave with the title, *Pine Island Stonehenge?* He pressed the screen on his phone and waited for the video to upload, then dialed a number from memory.

"Yeah," a voice said.

"I've got something I want to sell," Erik said. "I just posted a new video to my YouTube channel, but keep in mind the cave wasn't empty when I found it. I'll be in touch."

Erik didn't care about Anne, about the island or anything else they might find in the dirt. With any luck, the crystal stone he found would finance a new life on a tropical island somewhere far, far away.

***

Dylan stood at the summit of the hill, his body burning, chest heaving. He looked at the carnage that littered the ground around the stone altar. The blank, bloody stares of friend and foe mingled with the light of the full moon. Dylan dropped to his knees and let out a roar and his band of remaining comrades echoed in celebration.

"We've done it," said a heaving voice to his left. "Complete the circle."

He looked up into the canopy of trees and the stars beyond, then walked to the altar in the center of the stone circle. Its enormous capstone was bathed in the light of the moon.

His companions fanned out around him, beating their chests in unison with closed fists. Dylan began to speak and the capstone responded, glowing amber at first and then burning white hot.

Dylan, wake up.

"Dylan," Abigail repeated, "wake up."

Dylan stirred and then went rigid, unable to get a bearing on where he was. Face-down in a small, domed room, he couldn't see beyond a wall of light that surrounded everything. Abigail stood across from him, Constance and Margaret by her side. Her red hair was braided neatly into a single knot that lay across the grey shawl she wore over her shoulders.

She held out her hand and helped Dylan to a table and chair in the center of the room. They seemed to grow right out of the light, and their wooden construction looked more like the weathered trunk of an ancient tree than the work of a carpenter.

"What's going on?" Dylan asked.

Dylan's head ached and the pain in his shoulder pulsed down his arm into his fingertips. He reached for his flask, but it wasn't there.

"You're safe here, Dylan," Abigail said. "I hope you don't mind, but I decided it would be best if I cleaned you up. You, and your clothes."

"Cleaned up?"

"From your little, accident?" Abigail said. "Please don't be embarrassed – I leaked a little myself, truth be told – it's just that, time moves differently where I've brought you, and you would have had the worst rash by the time you woke up. Not to mention the smell, which in this confined space–"

"—Okay, yes," Dylan interrupted. "Thanks, for that. Truly."

Dylan looked around as his words were swallowed by the dim light of his surroundings.

"So, where is here, anyway?"

"We're underneath your favorite tree, Dylan – the willow across from Mary's grave." She ran her hand against the wall and sent rainbow colored waves in every direction. "That's where we are, but I've added a little extra protection to make sure that nothing bothers us for a while."

Dylan rubbed gingerly at his shoulder.

"What happened? Why did Mary attack me?"

"It wasn't Mary, it was a demon," she replied. "I imagine it's been hunting you for months, drawn to you by the same energy that allows me and my daughters to interact with you on this plane."

Dylan's face went from confused to stupid.

"Your energy – your aura – is like a beacon," she explained. "You're like a bright light in the middle of a dark forest, Dylan. Your sorrow is drawing attention to the special energy that you carry."

Abigail took Dylan by the hand. Her skin was soft, warm, and it seemed to spark with electricity. Dylan ran his hands across the knotty surface of the table and it moved with him, mimicking his movements and cradling his hands.

Maybe Kyle was right?

Maybe he was going crazy.

"I have no idea what you just said," Dylan said.

"Hmph," Abigail furrowed her crimson brows. "I suppose this is a lot for you to take in. Usually, we're born into the gift, taught the basics by our parents from a young age. Let's see..."

"Whoa, hold on a minute," Dylan said. "The gift? Taught by our parents?"

"I told you he doesn't know," Margaret said and punched her sister in the arm. "How could he not know, Mama?" She looked at Abigail and pointed at Dylan's chest. "The light is right there!"

Abigail looked at Dylan and sighed. She passed her hand across the gnarled roots that were supporting the stool Dylan sat on. "Trees are living, breathing things. Would you agree?"

"Sure."

"They communicate with the world around them all the time, Dylan. You just have to know how to speak their language."

"Okay?"

"The tree – this tree – has been talking to you for most of the year," Abigail continued, "awakening your inner power, connecting you to your gift, so you could grieve, heal and sort through your memories of Mary."

"The tree has been talking to me," Dylan repeated.

"That's where the images of Mary have been coming from," Abigail said.

"But, Mary was real," Dylan said. "She was there with me. I felt her, I touched her, I…"

"That's the power you carry, Dylan," Abigail said. "This tree has been helping you find Mary in your subconscious – in ways you couldn't otherwise – and taught you to manifest her."

"Aha!" Dylan pointed at Abigail in triumph. "But Mary was in my kitchen, too! Last time I checked, this tree wasn't in my living room, so how did Mary show up there?"

Dylan smirked at Abigail, expecting to wake up from his dream at any moment.

"The tree hasn't just been talking to you, Dylan, it's been teaching you," Abigail patiently repeated. "You've been learning how to interact with the universe in new ways. The tree didn't call Mary to your kitchen, Dylan, you did."

Dylan laughed.

"People like you and I have been called many things – druid, shaman, healer, witch – but the truth is that we're the light of the stars, caretakers that are part of an ancient connection that links all of creation, including this tiny little blip of time and space called Earth."

"So…I'm a witch…you have magical powers…and my dead wife wants to steal this little light of mine?" Dylan counted off with the fingers on his left hand.

"I suppose you could say that," Abigail wrinkled her nose affectionately. "But it's we – we have magical powers, and that wasn't your wife—"

"—wait," Dylan interrupted, "so what you're saying is that wasn't Mary at all? All this time, I haven't really been talking to her?"

Dylan was suddenly sad. He knew it wasn't exactly natural to talk to his dead wife, but he always thought that he was talking to her. The idea that all of this had been a trick of his mind, or that he was just being fattened up for a celestial slaughter made him feel helpless, used.

Abigail stood up as if to leave.

"Wait," Dylan said. "Please, I have so many more questions."

"My girls need my attention right now, Dylan. They've never been so close to a reaper, and that demon is not going to give up its prey so easily." She brushed back the hair from Dylan's brow and sighed. "Don't worry, we'll talk again, but right now you need to reconcile your feelings for Mary. I'll see you again soon."

Abigail took her girls by the hands and disappeared into the light at the edge of the room. As soon as they were gone, a book appeared on the table. Dylan recognized it immediately. It was the diary he had started when Mary got sick, the journal that chronicled the slow descent of their relationship into the murky haze of her mental illness. His final entry was the day of her funeral.

He had buried the journal with Mary.

Dylan shuddered as he realized what this room had in store for him.

***

Some residents of Pine Island brought cars with them on the ferry, but Anne followed her grandfather's example, filling the crate over the back wheel of her bike twice a week at the grocery store. Swinging her leg over the frame, she pushed away from the front porch of the cabin and began pedaling. The shade of the pines was welcome, since the cool breeze that had been coming off the lake didn't reach this far into the island.

Anne came to a fork in the road. The main road continued down to what everyone called The Junction, a small crossroads containing Collin's Grocery, Dagwood's Pub & Grub, and the post office. The grocery store was next, but first Anne had to keep her traditional beginning-of-summer appointment. She veered right at the crossroads and went up the hill toward the highest spot on the island, where Nancy lived.

Nancy McCoy was old money, and she was commonly considered the finest summer resident of Pine Island. She was a widow, the grandmother of Anne's ex-fiancé Steven, and a close friend of her grandfather's. Her grandfather would visit Nancy all summer long, and Anne always suspected they were more than friends, but neither her grandfather nor Nancy had ever said anything to confirm her suspicions.

As she reached the top of the hill, Nancy's house came into view. The forest had long ago been cleared back to allow sunlight to penetrate the estate. Her home was a shining example of Victorian Era craftsmanship and with her immaculate gardens, it looked like something out of a Jane Austen novel. Even this early in the summer, there were vibrant green shrubs surrounded by yellow, red and pink highlights. The home had belonged to her great-grandfather, a lumber baron who built a fortune in the 19th century. Subsequent generations grew the family's wealth in Chicago and Cleveland through various manufacturing and shipping interests before branching out into the venture capital and financial services that continued to subsidize her independence.

Anne parked her bike and rang the doorbell. Nancy's steward, Aiden opened the door and smiled.

"Nice to see you well, Miss Leahy," he said and stood aside. "She's waiting for you in the front room."

"I was beginning to think you had forgotten about me," Nancy said as Anne entered the room. "Come in, come in."

"Sorry, Mrs. McCoy, I had an unexpected visitor this morning," Anne replied. "I hope it's not too late for tea?"

"Mrs. McCoy? Something certainly has you rattled, child. You know I won't tolerate that kind of formality from you." Nancy gestured at the sofa. "Come on, dear," she smiled, "whatever it is, I'm sure it's no match for Earl Grey."

Nancy was dressed for company, but casual since it was Anne. As always, her grey, shoulder length hair was neatly tucked away in a bun.

Anne sat down and Aiden disappeared to prepare the tea service.

"Now then," Nancy said, "tell me about it while we wait for the kettle."

Where Celeste was a walking orgasm waiting to happen – Anne knew that her raucous sexuality was always simmering, just below the surface of any conversation – Nancy also had a fascination with Anne's love life for some reason. Maybe she was living vicariously through Anne, maybe it was because Anne had been engaged to *'her Steven,'* but their conversations always included something about Anne's current affairs of the heart.

She decided to lance the boil and get it over with.

"A scuba diver lost his boat," Anne said.

"A scuba diver? You don't see much of that around here," Nancy replied.

"I know," Anne said. "He was poking around the rocks on the east side of Grandpa's island."

Nancy stiffened.

"The east side of the island?"

"Yes," Anne replied. "He motored his boat into the inlet in front of the cottage, asked if he could use the bathroom, and well…" she trailed off.

Nancy recognized the look on Anne's face.

"He's handsome?"

Anne could feel her face getting warm as she pictured his tan skin, blonde hair, and muscular shoulders.

"Yes, but that's not the point," Anne said. "I mean, come on! I left a trail of defeated men twice as handsome and a thousand times more powerful than him scattered across boardrooms from New York to Beijing." Anne shook her head. "No, I'm just angry. Angry that he thought he could waltz into my life, turn on the charm, and get my permission for some sort of archaeological dig up on the hill."

"The hill?" Nancy said. "Really?"

"Really," Anne replied. "Apparently, he found some sort of cave with carvings while he was diving. He and the state archaeologist want to do an excavation, but I told him no, and I'm sure I'll never hear from him again."

"A cave," Nancy smiled, shook her head, and looked out the window.

"I mean – yeah – he's attractive," Anne said, starting to calm down, "and I suppose it did, sort of, maybe, make me realize how long it had been since..." she trailed off again.

"Relax, dear," Nancy said. "Aren't we past all of that?"

"Past what?" Anne asked.

"I don't hold you responsible for what happened between you and my Steven," Nancy said. "What's done is done. For whatever reason, you two just weren't meant to be together. Now, come on," she smiled, "does this scuba diver have a name?"

"Erik Larson," Anne said. "Not that it matters." Despite Nancy's acceptance, she decided it was time to change the subject. "So, how is Steven doing? Is he still in New York?"

Nancy gave her a narrow glance, but before she could respond, Aiden walked in with the tea service and set it on the table in front of the couch. The china was floral, ornate, and undoubtedly original. He offered Anne a scone from a small plate, which she took, and then poured each of them a cup of tea.

"Yes, he's still in New York," Nancy said. "And London, and Tuscany, and Dubai, and who knows where next. To tell you the truth, I'm not sure what has gotten into Steven lately. He's barely working, and it's just shameful the way he jets from one distraction to the next." Nancy scowled. "A man used to have something to show for his empire, something to be proud of, and he would find ways to give back to society. My great-grandfather would not approve of his behavior, of that I'm sure."

"I have to admit," Anne said, "there are parts of that life that I miss."

"Such as?" Nancy prodded.

"Not the money," Anne said. "I agree with you on that – fifteen years of empire building was enough for three lifetimes – but the energy, the thrill, the power. It was all such a rush."

Anne paused while Aiden poured Anne a cup of tea from the kettle.

"Sugar?"

"Not today, thank you," Anne replied and smiled at Aiden, who quietly left the room.

"You and Steven were quite a team," Nancy said.

"I know," Anne replied softly. "I can still remember the look on his face when I told him I wanted out. He didn't see it, and he probably still doesn't. The utter futility of that endless cycle of consumption. I was so out of control, Nancy, consumed by my desires, but with no direction, no balance."

"Money does provide certain comforts and security in life, dear," Nancy said. "It's allowing you to live here on the island, after all. My people in New York still ask about you, wonder if you're coming back into the fold."

"I'm sorry," Anne sighed, "you're right, and I didn't mean to preach. I certainly worked hard for what I earned, but it just wasn't enough. It was never going to be enough. I thought Steven would cash out with me, and we would just unplug from the world, spend our days thinking of new ways to please each other. But, well..."

"Your ears are red, dear," Nancy said.

"Really?" Anne touched her cheeks and felt the heat radiating from her ears. "Shit, I'm sorry."

Anne looked out the front window and her eyes locked on the delicate pink hues of the flowers outside. As they swayed gently in the breeze, she was reminded of the more basic rhythms of nature that had called her back. She was finding her balance being back here on the island – the fact that she could discuss her life in finance without cursing and slamming her fist on the table was certainly progress – but something continued to elude her, like a piece of her soul, whispering from the shadows, just out of reach.

"Well, enough of that," Nancy said curtly. "I didn't invite you here to discuss your ex-fiancé or boorish scuba divers," Nancy sat up formally in her chair. "This is our first tea of the summer, after all. Here's to bright skies, cool breezes and summer pleasures."

They both raised their cups and took a sip of the tea.

"So, how is your garden coming along this year?" Nancy asked.

"Just fine," Anne replied. "It never seems as lush or as vibrant as when grandpa was still here, but I do my best."

Anne took a small nibble from her scone and chewed politely.

"Well dear, he would be very proud of you for maintaining the cottage the way you have," Nancy said, "and now that you're here year-round, I'm sure you'll get a better handle on it."

Anne finished her tea and gently set the cup on the saucer.

"Thank you, Nancy. I hope you'll forgive me, but I really need to run so I can get some groceries before Mr. Collins closes up."

"Time is our friend, Anne," Nancy said, placing her cup gently on the saucer and setting it on the table. "And take it from a woman who has been alone longer than you've been alive – daylilies make for predictable bedfellows. I'll bet you feel better once you get your hands in the dirt."

Nancy stood up and walked with Anne to the foyer, where Aiden had already opened the front door. Anne thanked Nancy again, then got on her bike and pedaled down the driveway.

"We have a problem," Nancy said as Aiden shut the door.

"Yes?"

"His name is Erik Larson."

CHAPTER FIVE

Nancy was partly right; gardening was therapeutic. It was no accident that Anne's front yard was filled with boxes, planters and neat green rows, but Anne never considered it an outlet for lover's scorn (if it was, her garden was an epic monument of sexual frustration). She had always considered it more of a testament, a living legacy to her grandfather. He was the one that taught her about herbs, which ones would grow in the climate outside their front door, and their basic magical properties. Over the years, he helped her fine-tune her craft, incorporating the effects of her favorite herbs into her spells and intentions – not to mention her recipes.

No, the constant nurturing was not a chore to Anne, and today was no exception. It had been two weeks since Erik Larson had turned her summer upside down, but the heat of the sun and the sweat of her labor helped her cope with her new reality. She dug out a couple more weeds, ripped them apart lengthwise six times and then chopped them mercilessly with her trowel.

She walked over to the porch and took a sip of lemonade, then decided it was time to put some closure on Erik's deception. She fetched her bat from inside, then sat down on the steps and chiseled out another tick mark near the end. This was an honor usually reserved for people Anne had seen naked and aroused, but Erik had been in her bathroom with his dick in his hands, so she decided that was close enough. He was number nineteen. She put a coat of blood red nail polish on the fresh groove, and leaned it against the white railing to dry.

Anne was just getting back into her garden when her phone jolted to life, vibrating and chiming in her back pocket.

"Hey, Celeste," Anne said.

"Anne! OMG girl!" As usual, Celeste shouted through the phone. "You're famous! Well, I mean almost famous, they didn't mention you or anything, but I just saw the whole thing on YouTube! That video that went viral – it's your grandfather's island!"

"I know," Anne replied. "Crazy, right?"

"So how are you doing? Are you okay?"

"I guess so," Anne replied. "I mean, it's not something you can really prepare for."

"Have reporters been there yet?" Celeste asked.

"No, but I've had to chase away three boats this morning, and I saw a helicopter flying around. It's starting to get to be too much to handle." Anne looked up as a police car drove up to the end of the lane. Two men got out of the car and started walking toward her front gate. "Celeste, I gotta go. Someone's here."

"Alright, I'll call you later! It's probably a reporter! I'll look for you on TV!"

"Hello, Miss Leahy?" the man asked. He was a slight man, skinny and nearly bald. His lip quivered from behind a grey goatee beard. "I'm Dr. Jim Parsons, the state archaeologist. I thought I might trouble you for..."

Anne turned her back to him, got back down on the ground, and started digging again.

"...Sheriff?" Dr. Parsons said and turned to his companion.

"Miss Leahy? I'm Sheriff Tom Jenkins. Could we trouble you for a quick conversation?" He held up a badge and pointed at the front door. "Maybe out of the sun? Over on the porch?"

"If you want to tear up my grandfather's island, the answer is no." Anne replied, continuing to dig in the dirt.

"Miss Leahy, please," Dr. Parsons said. "I would have called you on the phone, but this is just too important. I had to talk to you face to face about what Erik found in that cave."

He waited for a response, but Anne just folded her arms.

"The markings on the wall are like nothing anyone has seen on this side of the Atlantic. It looks like something very ancient. We think the cave and whole hill above it were all connected, a ritual site of some sort, perhaps. I must impress upon you how vitally important it is that we study the markings, the cave, and the hill above them. If we find artifacts—"

"I said, no," Anne said without looking up.

"Miss Leahy, really. I'm here with a legitimate request on behalf of the archaeological community!"

Anne set down her trowel, stood up and wiped the sweat from her forehead with the back of her hand. He looked sincere, but she couldn't help but feel used – just like with Erik – and she could tell that she was losing control of the whole situation.

"You know, you're right," Anne said, "some people would probably jump at the chance to have you dig in their backyard. They'd probably love to get their hands dirty and put it all over their Facebook page."

"Exactly!" Dr. Parsons said.

"But that's not me." Anne sat down on the steps and eyed Dr. Parsons. "What's in it for you? Why do you want this so bad?"

"I admit, this is a once-in-a-lifetime opportunity for me. If only we had discovered this twenty years ago." He sighed. "But I assure you, you'll get full credit for all of your cooperation."

"Credit?" Anne sneered. "I don't care about getting credit! I just want to be left alone! My grandfather's island is special...it's..." she trailed off. Anne had learned to keep her spirituality to herself. Most people were too indoctrinated to understand the pagan roots of her religious beliefs, and she had decided that discretion was a virtue.

"Miss Leahy," Sheriff Jenkins said, waving a hand at Dr. Parsons. "I get how this must feel, but I'm not sure you understand what's going on here. This thing has taken on a life of its own." He scratched his head and looked at the footbridge over his shoulder. "I came over from the mainland where hundreds of people are queued up for the ferry. They tell me that if everyone who bought an electronic ticket actually shows up, they're going to have to run that ferry 24 hours a day for two straight weeks. I think you know they aren't coming to take a bike ride and go home. They're coming to see your hill and that stone ring."

"Well, I don't want them here," Anne said. "They need to respect my privacy."

"Those people have rights, too," Dr. Parson's chirped, "and so do the business owners that survive off them. You can't just turn people away from the ferry, or tell them they can't come to the island —"

"Ah, the almighty dollar," Anne said and shook her head. "You know, there's more to life than being rich and famous, Dr. Parsons. Maybe we should be talking about how I can press charges against Erik Larson for trespassing?"

"He said he had your permission to dive around the island," Dr. Parsons said, giving the Sheriff an anxious look.

"Yeah, but not until he already had what he wanted! Is he making money off that video of his?" Anne retorted. "It's funny, but I don't remember discussing how we would split YouTube's advertising revenue?"

"Look, you have a valid point, but I think you might want to focus more on how to handle your new celebrity status, Miss Leahy," the Sheriff continued. "This is becoming a very public event, and we're starting to get concerned about public safety. We're coordinating with the Eagleton police force and trying to get a plan in place on how to manage and control these people."

The Sheriff wiped the sweat from his forehead with the back of his hand.

"It would be a lot easier if you just let the archaeologists onto the hill," he said, "and allowed people to come for a quick visit."

Anne stood silent in the doorway. Having strangers traipse all over her grandfather's island was the last thing she wanted, but it was clear that saying no wasn't going to make it stop. She knew this was one of those moments in life, where decisions had already been made and plans were already in motion, and the best she could hope for was to find a way to manage the pain, to go with the flow.

"Miss Leahy?" the Sheriff pressed.

"Alright," she said softly. "You can screw around underwater all you want, but you're not digging up there until the summer is over."

Dr. Parsons shook his head in frustration.

"You don't understand. We have to start digging now!" The tip of his nose turned red. "This isn't an episode of *Time Team,* Miss Leahy. It could take us all summer, maybe more. We might need years to properly excavate the site and catalogue our finds. Not to mention, it's imperative that we get in there and do our work for the historical record before anyone else has a chance to mess with things."

"Years?" Anne's hands were shaking, and she felt her face getting warm. "Dr. Parsons, those rocks aren't going anywhere! You can either dig at the end of the summer, or you won't dig at all. Is that clear?"

"But, the two figures on the wall!" Dr. Parsons pleaded. "Don't you want to know their story? Who they are? What they did?"

Sheriff Jenkins raised his hand at Dr. Parsons and shook his head.

"Why don't you wait in the car for me, Dr. Parsons?" the Sheriff said, more command than question. He scanned Anne's garden as he watched him skulk away. "Your herbs look like they're coming in strong. My wife and I have a vegetable garden in my backyard, Miss Leahy, but all we seem to do is feed the deer."

Anne laughed through her nose and gave the Sheriff the hint of a smile as Dr. Parsons shut the passenger door to the police car. She appreciated the Sheriff's kindness, even if it was back handed.

"There's a man named Bryan who is taking responsibility for organizing the, uh, pilgrimage, as they're calling it," the Sheriff said. "He is going to check in with you and with me every day. If you have any issues, speak to him or you can call me directly. This has my cell phone number on it and you can call me anytime." The Sheriff handed Anne a business card. "Day or night."

"Thanks."

"Personally, I think they just want to howl at the moon a little, and I don't anticipate any serious trouble. Now about Dr. Parsons..." The Sheriff paused. "I would recommend you let him take care of his business this summer too. You know he isn't going to go away, especially with all the people around. If he wants to do some work on that hill, I think you should hear him out."

"Alright," Anne replied, "but I'm not making any promises."

"Fair enough," the Sheriff said. "We'll talk more about it once you've had a chance to get used to all this. If I were you, I'd get some rest. You're going to have a long day tomorrow."

As the Sheriff drove away, Anne went back to shredding weeds, cursing Erik Larson and his devilish blue eyes.

***

Dylan looked at the leather journal on the table with morbid curiosity, then sniffed. It had none of the odors you would expect after sharing a casket with a corpse for nearly a year. It sat on the table, the black velvet band still tied around it in a neat bow. He didn't understand why Abigail had insisted he read it, but he didn't have a choice. With two quick pulls, the ribbon fell away and Dylan fanned absently through the pages with his thumb. He stopped near the front at an entry with a lot of scribbles and writing in the margins.

He started to read:

I CAN'T BELIVE YOU TOLD ME TO GO FIND SOME HOTTIE AT THE BAR AND FUCK HER GOOD. Mary, I need you to understand that your words hurt me today. I can't even remember what set you things off, but I love you and care for you deeply. When you said that I should find someone else it broke my heart. It made me feel sick to my stomach. It made me sad. It made me want to go fuck some hottie at the bar!

"Describe your feelings, Dylan," the therapist had said, looking at him over his gaudy designer glasses. "You need to explore your feelings in this journal, and practice talking about them without placing blame." He had stopped to check the time on his watch, then said, "use this as a way to start..."

...mutually respectful dialogue. Fucking prick. Even now, Dylan wanted to plant that guy against the wall and slowly squeeze the light out of his world. He flipped further back in the journal and read on:

Mary, today you tried to hurt me, and it made me feel abandoned. I felt like You tried to hit me in the head with a cast iron skillet! You knocked a chunk out of the kitchen cabinet – what if that had been my skull?!!! Did you take your fucking meds today??? I don't understand why you won't get better – why can't they fix you? WHY CAN'T I FIX YOU!?

Mary had never wanted to take her meds. They were supposed to keep her on an even keel – set her mind to a constant neutral – so she wouldn't lose her grip on reality.

"I don't feel like myself when I take them," she explained one day.

Dylan thought that was kind of the *whole point* of taking them, but she always had an excuse. Eventually, she gave in and started taking them religiously. She made a big deal out of it, had Dylan supervise the process, and even had him inspect her gaping, empty mouth. But it didn't help. Even after Doctor Glasses increased her dosage, she was still prone to psychotic breaks with fits of rage and paranoia.

Dylan flopped the journal on the table and put his head in his hands. "I don't understand," he said out loud, "why do I have to read this?"

The silence of this place was not natural. He got up and walked over to the nearest wall.

"Hey!" he shouted, "I don't understand!" He pounded on the wall of light with both hands, but the slapping and thumping were quickly absorbed. "Answer me!" he shouted at the brightness, "I buried that fucking thing for a reason!"

Dylan sat down at the table, defeated. He needed a drink. His hands were shaking, and his head was pounding so hard that the back of his eyes ached. He buried his head in his forearm.

"*Why*?" Dylan spat the words into the table, "why are you doing this to me?"

Silence.

With a roar, Dylan grabbed the journal and threw it as hard as he could. It hit the curtain of light with a hollow thud and fell to the floor in a heap.

"I'm here, Dylan," Mary said.

She stood in the opposite corner of the room, her hands folded in front of her waist. The blood and bruises were gone, replaced by the delicate features he tried so desperately to remember her by. Her long black hair fell over her shoulders, her blue eyes sparkling above rosy cheeks. It was Mary – alive, breathing, whole – not the thing she had become.

"Mary? Is it really you?"

"It's really me."

He rushed to her, still shaking in frustration, and took her into his arms. He cradled her cheeks in his hands and kissed her lips. They were soft, her breath warm and moist. He kissed her cheek, her neck, her shoulder and laughed through the tears forming in his eyes.

"It's you," he said and lifted her into the air.

He spun her around, set her back down, then buried his head in her hair and hugged her tightly with both arms. He looked into her eyes, ran his fingertips down her cheek and tickled her behind the ear. Mary trapped his hand with her shoulder and giggled.

"Knock it off," she said and smiled.

"God, I miss that," Dylan said.

Dylan continued to touch her gently, tentatively. It had been so long since Mary had been herself that it almost felt like the first time. He ran his hands across her shoulders and down her arms, plunged them briefly below her hips and then up toward her chest.

"Dylan *Michael!*" Mary said and pushed his hands away. "Absolutely not!"

"I'm sorry," Dylan laughed, "it's just been so long, and it's you – it's *really* you." There was so much Dylan wanted to say to her, so many things he had experienced since she died that he wanted to share. Not to mention all his unanswered questions. "How is this possible, anyway?"

"I can't tell you that," Mary said. "What little you could understand, you wouldn't believe. But I'm here, really and truly." She ran her hand across the wall, sending shimmering blue waves in every direction. "Just think of this place as a cosmic coffee shop, a place where we can be together without the limitations of your reality holding us back."

"Uh...limitations of *my* reality? You're dead, Mary. That's a pretty big limitation." Dylan ran his hands through his hair. "And why can't it be a cosmic pub? I could really use a drink about right now."

Mary moved back to where Dylan was standing and looked him directly in the eyes.

"Drinking is not going to bring me back, Dylan."

"I know," he said defeated, "but it helps kill the pain. Every single day, I ask myself what I could have done differently. If there was something, anything I could have done to help you, to keep you safe, to keep you here with me. Why did you do it?" Dylan asked, unable to hide the hurt in his voice. "How could you give up on us?"

Mary looked over Dylan's shoulder, the pain in his eyes too much for her to bear.

"I," she started to say, then placed a hand over her mouth. She walked over to the table and gathered her thoughts. "Honestly, a lot from those last few months is pretty hazy. I don't remember everything, just bits and pieces, like a dream. But..." she trailed off, a faraway look on her face.

"But what?" Dylan pressed.

"But the images. I remember the images in my head," Mary said, "the violent, horrible, images."

"You never said anything about that," Dylan said, concerned. "Maybe they would have changed your medications or your therapy. Why didn't you say something?"

"I tried," she said, "but I couldn't. The words weren't there to describe it. They started off as dreams, but then I started getting them all the time, and I didn't know what was real and what was just in my head. That day," she looked at the wall of light, "I was trying to escape, to get away from the terrible urges I was having. I was starting to lose control, Dylan, and I was afraid that I would do those horrible things to you."

A tear ran down her cheek, and Dylan brushed it away.

"What horrible things?" he asked.

"I can't..." she hesitated. "I can't say, Dylan. I honestly don't remember, but I know that's why I..." she stopped, unable to say the words.

Dylan pulled her close, buried her head in his shoulder and they wept, together. He continued to hold her as the moments passed, as all the months of doubt and guilt came rushing out with his tears, released at last.

"I love you, Mary," he said and brushed her tears with his thumbs.

"And I love you," Mary replied, gently kissing his away.

"This is so fantastic," Dylan said, "I don't know how this is possible, but all I care about is that I can see you. How will you know when I'm around? Should I send some sort of signal or something?"

Mary kissed him on the cheek without responding and picked the journal off the floor.

"How?" Dylan persisted. "How will I see you again?"

She flipped to the last entry and held out the journal. "I need you to read it to me, Dylan." When he didn't take it from her, she put it in his hand. "*You* need to read it to me, Dylan."

Dylan looked at the journal. Mary had opened it to the last page with writing. It was the final message Dylan had written before he buried the journal with his wife. He couldn't remember the words, but he knew what it said. Saying goodbye to Mary was the most difficult thing he had ever done. He scanned the page and let out a sigh, then read it aloud:

My dearest Mary,

You left without saying goodbye.

I blame myself.

I am putting your body in the ground, but your spirit will live with me forever.

-Dylan

"I didn't know what to say," Dylan said, "but I had to try."

He gently set the journal back on the table.

"I know," said Mary, "and those words are the reason we're here right now. Your words – your intentions – woke up something special inside of you. You're special, Dylan, and you have a special purpose, but you won't be able to follow your path as long as I'm holding you back."

Mary smiled and took Dylan by the hand.

"I love you, Dylan, but you need to let go." She put a small piece of wood in his hand and kissed him on the forehead. "Goodbye, Dylan."

"No, wait!"

Dylan reached for her, but in an instant, she was gone. He slumped to his knees and began to cry again. He was still weeping when Abigail and her girls reappeared.

"Why are you torturing me?" Dylan asked, wiping his eyes. "Am I dead? Is this Hell or something?"

"No, Dylan, this isn't Hell," Abigail said.

"Why was Mary here? Can you please tell me what's going on?"

"Mary was right," Abigail placed a hand on Dylan's shoulder, "you're—"

"—don't you dare say I'm fucking special!"

Constance gasped.

Abigail sighed.

"Should I conjure up some soap, Mommy?" Margaret asked.

"No, Mr. Ward has taken in a lot," Abigail calmly replied. She raised her eyebrow and Dylan felt a gentle but obvious pressure in his groin. "We'll give him a pass – *just this once*."

"Sorry," Dylan quickly said, looking at Constance and Margaret, "it's just – all I really care about is being able to see Mary. That's all I've wanted, ever since...she died. Do you at least know where she went?"

"I'm sorry, Dylan, no," Abigail said. "I can't see into the outer realms where she is. Our existence is confined to the cemetery." Abigail helped Dylan sit up. "Mary contacted *me.* She got here just before the reaper attacked and told me she had a message for you."

"I guess I need some time to process all of this." Dylan looked at the piece of wood in his hand and put it in his pocket. "Can I please go home, now?"

"First, you need to rest," Abigail said and gestured at the floor.

The roots of the willow tree came up out of the ground under Dylan, creating a bed that gently conformed to his body. As the roots wrapped around him, Dylan felt a wave of peace and safety wash over him, and Mary appeared again across the room. She whispered something to Abigail that made her smile and then kissed each of the girls on the forehead.

Mary's smiling face was the last thing Dylan saw as the darkness closed in. He couldn't help but feel suspicious – that there was something that Mary and Abigail weren't telling him – but sleep was calling. Gentle, peaceful sleep.

Whatever it was, it could wait until tomorrow.

CHAPTER SIX

Anne pushed her way through the crowd at the top of the hill, where the smell of long-overdue showers mingled with the sweet twang of marijuana and cheap beer. This arrangement had turned out to be more than she bargained for, but she couldn't do much about it now. They had only been diving a few days before Dr. Parsons returned to ask about excavating the hill, but Anne held firm. They were doing exploratory work above ground, but hadn't opened any trenches. It had been six weeks now since he started his work, graciously including any and all visitors to help with the initial survey. His minions had even started a twitter feed to keep everyone updated on the latest finds.

Anne closed her eyes and took a long, deep breath. Just a few more weeks until their crazy little party, and then Anne could salvage what was left of her summer.

Ahead on the summit of the hill, the crowd gathered to listen to a young girl who was strumming an acoustic guitar. She sat on one of the stones, her head swaying and her eyes closed. Anne couldn't make out the words, but the girl's voice was sweet and the tune was warm and familiar. Couples swayed together, some holding hands, others kissing. The ringleader, Bryan, was standing next to the giant Oak tree and his face brightened when he saw Anne.

"Hey, little Annie," he smiled and waved.

Anne stopped and took it all in. Coolers creaked open and shut, and the sound of rattling ice echoed through the trees.

This is wrong, she thought.

She rubbed her temples and shut her eyes, but the sound of Erik Larson's voice made it impossible to escape.

"We ready to go, or what?" Erik asked a man behind a camera.

"We're rolling, big man."

"Hey, guys!" Erik said to the camera and clapped his hands. "You'll never believe it, but I ran into a couple people who hadn't seen my video yet, and they have a few questions for me today." He gestured at the gaggle of young women surrounding him. They all wore the same bright purple t-shirt with the *Lefty's Energy Drink* logo stretched across their chests. "But, before we get started, I have to say thanks again to all my patrons over at Patreon for their awesome support. Thanks to you, I was able to hire someone to shoot and edit my videos! Now I can spend more time unlocking all the secrets up here. Thanks, guys!"

"Alright, ladies, I don't want to judge, but as of this morning, my video notched over 15 million views. I'm not sure how you missed that!" Erik looked back at the camera. "I guess it's hard to tell if this is about history, or if it's just one continuous party up here. Either way, you've got to come here and check it out, and next week would be the perfect time!" He walked over to the camera and pulled out a handful of cash. "Each day next week, we're doing a $10,000 *History's Mysteries* giveaway to one lucky camper up here. Five days, ten-thousand dollars, but you gotta be here to win!"

Erik shot a pretend bullet at the camera with his finger, then walked back to girls and put his arm around the first one in line.

"So, isn't diving, like, dangerous?" the girl asked, right on cue.

"Sure, it is, but knowing that I'm the first person to see something in thousands of years makes it worth the risks."

"I'd love to do what you do," said another, flipping her hair over her shoulder. "Did you have to go to college?"

"Some people waste their money on college, but I learned everything I know from hard work and experience. I have lots of experience." He winked at the girl and then checked the enormous black dive watch on his wrist. "Alright, guys, I'm super stoked because I have an interview with the local TV station. So, I'm gonna go do that real quick, but stick around and we'll finish up today's video with an update on something really amazing. You're not even gonna believe what we found this morning!

While I'm doing that, go ahead and comment below on what you think we found, and make sure you smash the like button, subscribe, and ring that bell! I'll be right back!"

"Miss Leahy, over here!" Anne recognized the voice of Dr. Parsons. He leaned against one of the stones, scribbling in a notebook. "Thanks for agreeing to see me. This really will be a lot easier if I can show you what I'm talking about."

"No problem," Anne lied.

She choked down the Erik Larson-induced bile creeping into the back of her throat, and gave Dr. Parsons a forced smile.

"Now, I know it's hard since they're scattered all over the ground, but we've been working on mapping out what the stones would have looked like when they were still upright. You see here, how the stones are in a circular pattern?"

He waited for Anne to acknowledge his question.

"Yes?" Anne replied with fake interest.

"They form an outer ring, like a boundary. Now, we used ground penetrating radar to see what was beneath the ground here inside the circle," he gestured at the ground with his hand in a circular motion, "and guess what?"

Again, he waited.

"What?" Anne was losing patience.

"There is what looks like a set of stone steps leading down into the cave below. Our divers found a natural place for a stairway, but it was backfilled with rock and sediment. It confirms what we suspected all along! Whatever went on up here was absolutely linked to the cave and the altar below!"

Anne didn't think it was possible, but his smile seemed to get even larger.

"That's great," she said and turned to leave.

"No, wait, there's more," he said. "We won't know for sure until we excavate, but we've mapped everything out with GPS and we'll be running it through some computer models back at the lab. I think the whole site is designed as some sort of celestial marker, to highlight celestial events and the passage of time. The capstone is on the east side of the circle, and the cave opens to the east, so we suspect there was some sort of alignment based on the rising sun at different times of the year. It reminds me of the Neolithic passage tombs, but I'm consulting with some colleagues to be sure. We've also got linguists working on the symbols that are on each of the stones – that's the key for us right now – we need to unravel them to be able to understand the context and the purpose for the site."

He finally stopped to breathe.

"Thank you, Dr. Parsons," Anne said patiently, "I appreciate you taking the time to show me this and explain it."

She didn't have the heart to tell him that Bryan had already told her everything. In theory, that was the whole point of the little gathering they were planning – to celebrate the celestial energy or something like that – but in practice, it seemed more like an excuse to party.

"It sets us up nicely for next season," Dr. Parsons continued, "when we can restrict public access and start excavating. Some of the stones up here were deliberately dumped over the cliff at some point, probably when they buried the cave. It's like someone wanted to hide this place. We may never know why, but we need to dig in the dirt, and hopefully, we will find some artifacts that will –"

"Thank you," Anne interrupted, "really."

"You'll have to excuse us, Dr. Jekyll. We have a lunch date!"

Anne turned around just as Celeste emerged onto the hill. She ran directly at Anne, a five-foot blur of brunette fury, and emitted a high-pitched squeal that made Dr. Parsons grab his ears in protest. They hugged and Celeste laughed in his face.

Finally, Anne had a friend to help her navigate this craziness.

"As Miss Leahy's trusted assistant, it is my duty to inform you that she is busy for the remainder of the afternoon – and this evening – plus, tomorrow." Celeste grinned and put her arm around Anne's shoulder. "Buh-bye."

"I'm so glad you're here," Anne said and led her friend down the path.

They waited when they got to the footbridge for a group of young kids to make their way across.

"Hey," said one of the girls to her companions as they passed, "I think that's her. Hi, Lady Leahy!"

Anne hated the nickname the island rats had given her. The kids all waved while Anne gave them the stink eye, then walked up the path into the trees.

"Lady Leahy?" Celeste rolled her eyes.

"Come on," Anne said, "I'm hungry."

They walked down the road toward the crossroads. Gunther Magnusson ran the finest (and only) eatery on this end of the island. It was pub grub at its finest, complete with a horseshoe-shaped tiki bar on the back patio where folk bands would sing for local and tourist alike. They made their way over to the bar where Gunther was slinging cocktails. When he saw Anne and Celeste, he took the drinks of two young men and moved them to the end of the bar.

"Get up," he told them in a deep voice.

The *'what the fuck'* looks on their faces quickly disappeared when Gunther walked around the bar. He was built somewhere between a linebacker and a professional wrestler, and the t-shirt he was wearing seemed about to burst from the combined girth of his pecs and biceps. They took their drinks and stood aside as Gunther laid a hug on Anne.

"How are you holding up, sweetie?" he asked.

"Alright," she said. "About as well as can be expected, anyway. You remember my friend, Celeste, right?"

"Sure, I do," he smiled. "Still got her picture on the wall of fame for drinking an entire Island Hurricane by herself."

"If you're going to fly, you might as well soar, I always say," Celeste smiled. "Speaking of which, how about a couple of hard ciders to get us started?"

"Sure thing," he replied, resuming his post behind the bar. He poured the drinks and set them down. "Want something to eat?"

"I'll have a club sandwich with the sweet potato fries," Anne said, and Celeste ordered the same.

"You got it," Gunther said and walked away to check on some customers at the other side of the bar.

"So, that guy Erik turned out to be a dick, huh?" Celeste asked.

"Pretty much," Anne said. "He's only in it for the attention and the money. He's made that abundantly clear."

"Did you really flash the shotgun when you chased him off?"

"Fuck, yeah, I did."

"Alright," Celeste said, holding up her drink. "So, fuck him! There's plenty of other options on the island right now." She clinked Anne's glass, even though it was still on the counter. She looked at the men Gunther had displaced and then scanned the crowd for a more suitable target.

"Yeah, if you're into guys who apparently have no job or other grown-up responsibilities," Anne replied.

"Oh, listen to you, little miss run away to live by yourself." Celeste's gaze locked on a man with dark hair, tan skin and designer sunglasses. "Yum. You don't look like that without money."

"You know what I mean," Anne said, ignoring the man as he smiled at them. "I just wish this summer was over."

"Well, I'm only here for a couple days, so you better be up for some fun," Celeste said and went over to say hello.

The band began to play, and Anne sat alone listening until their food arrived. She ate her sandwich, while Celeste ignored her lunch to flirt with the man at the end of the bar. Gunther replaced Anne's untouched cider with a pink lemonade.

"This summer will end eventually, right?" she asked.

"Hang in there, Anne. It'll feel better when it stops hurting."

He squeezed her shoulder and walked away.

***

The next thing Dylan remembered, he was standing outside his apartment, but when he put his key into the door, it wouldn't budge. He grabbed the handle and rattled it until the whole door shook.

"What the fuck?" Dylan whispered.

Dylan heard footsteps inside and the door opened until the security chain maxed out.

"Can I help you?" asked a young woman through the cracked door.

"I live here, but my key isn't working for some reason. Who are you?" Dylan asked.

"Uhm...actually, I live here," she replied. "Since last month."

She looked at Dylan more closely.

"Are you the guy that used to live here? With the wife that..." she stopped. "Look, I'm really sorry, but they evicted you. You'll have to talk to the landlord."

"But, my stuff – where is all my stuff?"

"I don't know, but it's not in here. You'll have to talk to the landlord," she repeated and shut the door.

Dylan walked out of the apartment building and onto the sidewalk leading down the bluff to the bay. He took out his cell phone to call his landlord, but the battery was dead. The only other things in his pockets were his keys (useless), his wallet (empty), and the piece of wood that Mary had given him.

Dylan skirted downtown, staying away from the water and the throngs of people that clogged the gift shops, coffee houses, and watersports outfitters. He wandered instead into the tree-lined Victorian neighborhoods that stretched for about ten blocks away from the water. For someone who was homeless and confused, he was surprisingly calm.

His encounters with Mary usually left him conflicted and desperate, but today he felt different – better than he had in years.

Kyle's rusted red pickup truck was in the driveway when Dylan got there. He had no idea what day it was, let alone what day of the week, but if Kyle's pickup was in the driveway, he had to be home.

Dylan rang the bell and waited. He heard muffled profanities from behind the door and then it swung open.

"Dylan?" Kyle shoved open the screen door and grabbed Dylan by the shirt. "Where in the fuck have you been?"

"I..." Dylan trailed off, unable to think of something believable.

Kyle started to say something with a pointed finger, then looked at the ground with pursed lips. He shook his head and released his grip.

"You hungry?"

"I am," Dylan said.

"Well, don't just stand there, come in."

Dylan stepped through the front door and waited for his friend to lead him into the kitchen.

"Chili dog?"

"Sure," Dylan said and sat down at the kitchen table.

Kyle put two hot dogs in a pasta bowl, opened a can of prepared chili, and dumped it on top. He hit a few buttons on the microwave, then leaned against the counter with arms folded and looked at his friend.

"It's been three months, Dylan!" Kyle exploded, unable to hold back his rage. "Are you fucking kidding me? No goodbye, no explanation. Just gone, for three months?"

"Did you say three months?" Dylan asked.

"Yeah, three months." Kyle shook his head and looked at the ceiling. "Edy thinks they'll find your body in some field with your head blown off."

"No, it was nothing like that. I just needed some time away," Dylan managed and looked down at the table.

"You've always been a terrible liar," Kyle said.

The bell on the microwave saved Dylan from responding to the accusation. Kyle retrieved the plate from the microwave, grabbed a fork and set the meal in front of Dylan with a clank. Dylan looked down at the steaming plate of mystery meats, and Kyle seemed to notice it for the first time.

"Sorry, man," he said. "You know how I am about cooking at home."

"No problem, it actually smells really good."

As Dylan tore into the hot dog with a fork, Kyle opened the fridge and offered his friend a beer.

"No thanks," said Dylan, "can I have some water?"

"Sure," Kyle said suspiciously, filling a glass and putting it on the table. He took a sip of beer and sat down across from Dylan.

The piece of wood that Mary had given him was poking his leg through his pants, so he took it out of his pocket and set it on the table. When Kyle saw the piece of wood, his shoulders slumped.

"Ah, Jesus," he said accusingly, "is that where you've been?"

"What are you talking about?" Dylan replied through a mouthful of chili.

"The totem, Dylan," he said, pointing at the piece of wood. "Those are the symbols they found at that place on Pine Island. It's been all over the internet and social media. The wannabe hippies have been camped out up there for most of the summer, having some sort of henge-a-palooza."

"I might have heard something about that, yeah," Dylan said and shoveled another pile of food into his mouth.

"Are you kidding me? Haven't you seen the video?"

Kyle pulled his phone out of his pocket, punched a few buttons, and set it on the table where Dylan could see the screen. Dylan took another bite and watched the video shot by Erik Larson. He saw the entrance to the cave take shape, the tunnel leading to the altar and each of the markings on the stone wall. The markings on the wooden totem that

Mary had given him were a perfect match to what was on Kyle's phone. Whatever 'special' meant, it clearly had something to do with the island.

As the video finished, Dylan sat in silence, then took another bite of his chili dog.

"So, if you weren't on the island, then where were you?" Kyle asked, looking at his friend with a raised eyebrow. "What happened?"

Dylan looked up from his plate and chewed in silence. Kyle tolerated Dylan's obsession with Mary, but there was no way he could tell him about Abigail and the demon. He barely understood himself. And three months? It felt more like a couple of days to him. He couldn't remember how he ended up back at his apartment, but he felt like he had just woke up from the night before.

Dylan decided it would be better to avoid unnecessary details, so he kept chewing in silence.

"Alright, when you're ready, I'm here," Kyle said. "Whatever you've been up to, it looks like it's been good for you. You don't look tired and you've put some weight back on."

"Yeah," said Dylan, pushing away his empty plate, "I feel better than I have in a long time."

"So, what's going on? Are you back in town? Do you have a place to stay?"

"Not exactly."

"Well, you're not staying at your old apartment, I can tell you that much. That money-grubbing son-of-a-bitch landlord had an eviction notice on your door the day after your rent was due," Kyle fumed. "Edy and I went over when your stuff was put on the curb and grabbed what would fit into my truck. It's still in the garage. Edy wouldn't let me get rid of it yet."

"I really appreciate that," Dylan said. "I didn't expect to be gone so long."

"Yeah, well, you're welcome to the couch in the office," Kyle said and stabbed his cell phone. "I'll let Edy know you're going to be here. She's gonna flip."

"Kyle, look, I'm..." Dylan struggled to find words. "Thanks."

"Not so fast. When Edy gets home, she'll probably beat the ever-loving shit out of you. She's not as refined and polite as I am."

Kyle was right; Edy was pissed. The first thing she did was haul off and hit Dylan in the shoulder with her left fist, before following up with her right square in his chest. During Dylan's continued non-explanation, she further vented her frustration with the nearest weapon she could find (a neon orange rubber spatula), hitting Dylan repeatedly on top of the head, and cursing wildly.

It was good to have friends.

The next day, Kyle started another sixteen-hour day at the restaurant, and Edy left to work her shift at the hospital. Dylan walked around to the side of the detached garage and opened the door. Everything he still owned was inside boxes stacked against the wall. He found a box with some clean clothes, grabbed a fresh pair of dark jeans and a black t-shirt, then went inside to take a shower. He couldn't take a ride on the ferry smelling like a hobo.

After he was fresh again, he grabbed a pen and scribbled a message on the back of an envelope sitting on the kitchen counter.

Thanks for everything.

I'm going to the island.

Back soon.

--Dylan

Dylan left the envelope on the counter and walked out the door. He headed toward the lake, walked until he reached Front Street, then followed it north along the shoreline until he got to the ferry dock. A burly man came up to Dylan.

"That's $40 for the crossing," he said mechanically. "Save your ticket and you can get return passage for $20."

Dylan reached for his wallet.

"Shit," he said.

The man looked at Dylan and then rolled his eyes. "Let me guess," he said. "You don't have the money, but it's *really* important you get to the island. It's like, a life-changing event, right man?"

"It's okay, Big D, he's with me," said a man over Dylan's shoulder.

The ticket man turned and scowled.

"You're due for a payment," he said. "People have been asking for more." He gave Dylan an uneasy glance. "Friday," he said, then ambled over to the next person in line.

"Hey, I'm Bryan," the man said walking over to Dylan.

"Dylan."

"Don't let old Richard scare you. He's cool. We have an arrangement," he winked and scratched his scraggly blonde beard. "He helps me share the island with people like you, and I help him with his retirement fund through a little side business of mine."

The cologne emanating from Bryan did little to mask the smell of marijuana.

"You're coming over just in time for the party on the hill this Saturday. If you're planning to stick around, the sheriff lets us stay in a tent city by the park because we don't cause trouble." Bryan looked at Dylan. "You're not looking to cause trouble, are you?"

"No," Dylan replied. "I'm just here to see what all the fuss is about, right?"

"Right." Bryan nodded.

"You said there's a party on Saturday?" Dylan asked.

"Yeah," Bryan said.

"What day is it today?"

Bryan laughed.

"You're gonna fit in just fine, Dylan," he said and walked away.

Instead of watching the island get closer, Dylan's eyes were drawn to the open waters of Lake Huron. Part of him wanted to jump overboard and swim away. Sure, he would get tired, succumb to hypothermia, then drown, but at least he would know what was going to happen. Not knowing what was on the hill – or why he was supposed to go there – made Dylan nervous.

The ferry blasted its horn and the Pine Island dock came into view.

"Come on," Bryan said, grabbing Dylan's arm. "I'll show you around."

The tent city looked like a campground on the Fourth of July, with tents, gear, and campfires all going gangbusters. A young girl sat on a picnic table strumming an acoustic guitar as they arrived. Her long blonde hair was pulled over her right shoulder, and Dylan guessed she weighed a hundred pounds soaking wet. Her tan contrasted sharply with the white bikini top she wore over blue jean shorts. She looked up as Bryan approached.

"Hey, you," she said sweetly to Bryan. "Who's the new guy?"

"Cindy, Dylan. Dylan, Cindy. Dylan is here to see what all the fuss is about. Did I get that right, Dylan?" Bryan looked at him, waiting for confirmation.

"Right," Dylan said. "I'm just here to see the hill like everyone else."

Cindy smiled, set down her guitar and stood up. Her eyes scanned Dylan up and down like a prize she had just won.

"Well, Dylan, things are pretty free around here. As long as you follow the golden rule, you're welcome to stay. Do unto others…." She ran her hand across Dylan's shoulder. "It looks like you're traveling light, so if you need a tent and a warm sleeping bag, you're welcome to share mine."

"Alright, Cindy," Bryan interrupted, tugging Dylan's shirt. "Come on, Dylan. Let's get some grub."

Cindy went back to her perch on the picnic table and started strumming the intro to *Hotel California*. Bryan led Dylan over to a group of picnic tables that were set up like a mess hall. A charcoal grill nearby was smoking, and the smell of grilled flesh made Dylan realize how hungry he was.

"We've got fresh vegetables if you're vegetarian or organic," Bryan said, "but there's plenty of meat and potatoes, too."

"Yeah, no," Dylan said and pointed at the grill, "whatever that is, I want it."

"Good deal. Hey everybody, this is Dylan." Bryan waited for the smattering of replies and greetings. "Alright, Dylan. Let me know if you need anything. And don't let Cindy put you off. We're not some kind of sex cult. There are plenty of empty tents and gear. Just find one that hasn't been claimed and put your backpack in it. That said, nobody's gonna judge if you decide to take her up on her offer. Glad you're here, Dylan." Bryan smiled, filled a plate and disappeared into a nearby tent.

He wasn't sure what he ate, but it was more than he expected under the circumstances, and it didn't take long for Dylan to find a solitary tent and settle in. He was still anxious about going up the hill, but a full stomach, the sounds of laughter and crackling campfires outside his tent, helped soothe him.

He didn't know what was on the hill or why he was special, but tomorrow, he intended to find out.

CHAPTER SEVEN

Dylan didn't own a gun, but he recognized the sound of the shotgun pumping behind him. Anne stood on the trail with her feet firmly planted, ready to shoulder the weapon quickly if Dylan gave her cause.

"Whoa," Dylan said, raising his arms. "I'm not looking for any trouble."

"I know what you're looking for," Anne said curtly. "There's only one way onto this island by foot, and it goes right by my front door and the 'no trespassing' sign I put up to keep you people out." She took a few tentative steps toward Dylan. "We're going to walk back down the path and you're going back to the camp in Grant Park. Got it?" Anne motioned with her head for Dylan to start moving.

"No, you don't understand," Dylan said.

"Don't understand?" Anne interrupted. "I've been chasing off your friends non-stop for the last three days! Here to connect with the positive energy of the universe?" she asked sarcastically. "Hoping to align your inner chi with the cosmic flow of goodness? I can smell the marijuana on you from here."

"What?" Dylan sniffed his shirt.

Fuck if she wasn't right.

"Look, like I said, I'm not trying to cause any trouble. I'm sorry, I should have knocked on your door, but they told me you wouldn't let me up there no matter what I said."

"See?" Anne shouted. "You *are* one of them! Nobody is supposed to be up here until the weekend, now move it!"

"No, please," Dylan pleaded, sitting down on the path. He put his face in his hands.

"Look, whatever you're looking for, it's not up there." Anne's tone lost some of its edge. "It's just a bunch of rocks," she lied.

Dylan started to respond, but instead he got up and slowly started walking down the hill. He kept his arms raised slightly and gave Anne plenty of room. This wasn't right. He needed to see what was on the hill.

It wasn't until he was across the footbridge that he stopped and turned around to face her. As he looked into her eyes, something happened. Dylan felt like the world was turning inside out, and images began flashing one after the other inside his head. Glimpses of Anne took shape. Her hair was down, spilling out of a dark hood covering her head. There was a blinding flash of light and then he saw Anne reaching for him, blood on her hands, her face dirty and intense. She was shouting, pleading with someone next to her.

Then suddenly it was over, and Dylan found himself looking into the barrel of the shotgun. Anne stood a few feet away from him, wide-eyed and shaking.

"Get away from me," she said and motioned toward the dirt road leading away from her cottage. "Now."

"Wait – what just happened?" Dylan asked.

"I'm serious." Anne replied. "Leave!"

Dylan turned and began walking away. For some reason, his heart ached. He didn't know why, but this just felt wrong. He knew he shouldn't be leaving, that he and Anne had some sort of connection that could help him figure out what Mary had told him. He knew this was where he was supposed to be.

"Wait," Anne said.

Dylan turned around and she lowered the shotgun, her face confused and distant.

"You were lying on the ground," Anne said. "You were bleeding. I had blood –"

"You had blood all over your hands," Dylan finished her thought.

"It was you," she said, "it was your blood. You were lying on the ground and I was holding your head in my hands. I could feel the breeze and smell the lake. I know it. I know it as sure as I'm standing here that we were on my grandfather's island. On the hill."

She took two steps back on the footbridge and lowered the shotgun.

"Who are you?"

"Dylan."

Anne hesitated. She wanted to tell Dylan to go away, like everyone else, but something kept the words from forming. There was no way she was going to invite him in for a chat after what just happened, but still...

"Come back after the party this weekend," Anne said. "We'll talk then."

Anne watched while he walked up the road, then went into the cottage and shut the door.

***

People clapped, hooted and hollered as Dylan walked back into camp.

"I told you he'd strike out," said a man sitting next to Cindy. "You owe me five bucks, Doogie!"

"Fuck off," someone groaned from a nearby tent.

Dylan picked an empty spot and slumped down on a picnic bench. He didn't sit long before Bryan walked over and joined him.

"You didn't tell me she had a gun."

"Awe, Little Annie is harmless," Bryan said. "You gotta understand, she's had a lot of people up there, dude. There's been a constant stream of short-timers, just here for a couple of days, maybe a long weekend. She used to let us camp out up there, but it got to be too much for her."

Dylan stared at the campfire without responding.

"Come on, Dylan," Bryan punched his shoulder, "you'll see everything and then some this weekend."

"Two days seems like a long time to me right now," Dylan said.

"I hear ya, but this is the best time to see the hill, man." Bryan gestured at the tents around him, "Right now, only the people who really care about what this place means are still here. Most have quit their jobs, ignored their bills, and walked away from their lives completely. A few are independently wealthy, and some are looking for meaning in their lives, but the one thing we all have in common, Dylan, is that we just want to be part of something bigger than ourselves."

"Yeah, I get that," Dylan said, pulling the totem from the front pocket of his blue jeans. He rubbed it between his thumb and first finger and stared at the markings by the light of the fire.

"Nobody knows what they say," Bryan said and pointed at the totem. "The archaeologist said we might never know what the symbols mean, without a Rosetta stone or something like they had for the hieroglyphs in Egypt."

They look familiar to me, Dylan thought to himself. The symbols were strung together in a line, but in Dylan's head he combined them into a three-dimensional pattern. He couldn't tell what it was, but a strange phrase began to echo in his head. He'd heard the same phrase when he met Anne earlier that night. He could see her flushed cheeks, the despair in her eyes, and hear this phrase, repeating loudly in his head.

"It's a special place, Dylan. No worries, I'll give you a guided tour myself in a couple days." Bryan got up and walked away.

Fuck special, Dylan thought, and got up to go to bed.

***

Anne took the kettle off the stove and poured the steaming water into her cup, where a stress-relief blend of chamomile, skullcap, vanilla, cloves and cinnamon waited to steep. She'd been chasing people away for so long that chasing Dylan off was almost second nature, but the connection she felt to him was uncanny. She had recognized his voice immediately, because she'd heard it before up on the hill, but it was more than that. It was like she already knew him.

Just the same, she needed some time to process what had just happened. She'd had visions before, but only in her dreams and they were never so vivid. They were always fuzzy, open to interpretation, thought and further meditation. There was nothing cryptic about the image she'd seen when she met Dylan, but it was the violence that really unsettled her. She'd never associated conflict of any kind with the hill or the stone circle.

Anne lit the candle on her coffee table and then settled into the couch. She spent a few minutes trying to shed the negativity of her encounter with Dylan, sipping her tea and watching the orange flame. After the anxiety dissipated, she took a few more deep breaths, opened her grandfather's grimoire, then flipped through the pages until she found what she was looking for – a diagram of the hill, with each stone labeled with its corresponding symbol. In the vision, the stones and their symbols were all shimmering a bright white, and a low pulse was humming in her ears.

Anne couldn't remember her grandfather ever talking about it with her, and he hadn't left any clues on the page. There were no lines coming off the stones indicating light, no notes in the margin hinting that he had ever seen them glowing.

Anne didn't know what the vision meant, but it was clear that the hill had secrets.

***

It wasn't the first time Erik had sold something from his treasure hunting, but it was the first time the buyer met him in person. He squinted at the tinted window of the black sedan and fingered the stone in the pocket of his shorts. Erik's associate had several buyers on the line, and he swore that Erik would regret cutting him out of the deal –

something about painful consequences – but why share? His internet fame had spread beyond his wildest expectations, and the buyer had contacted him directly. There was no reason to cut into his dream fund.

A young woman with blue hair and a piercing above her right eye got out of the front of the car, opened the passenger door and motioned for Erik to get in. The woman sitting next to him was wearing a crimson dress with dark sunglasses, and her blonde hair was wrapped around her neck, falling seductively across her left shoulder.

"The crystal, please," the woman replied and held out her hand.

Erik pulled it out of his pocket and handed it to her. The woman put it gently into a velvet container and gave Erik a large manila envelope. He tore it open and grinned at the stacks of $100 bills.

"Please, don't insult me by trying to count it," the woman said and gestured at the window. The door opened and the chauffer invited Erik to get out.

Erik was happy to oblige.

He was still smiling and thumbing through the envelope when the black sedan disappeared. He went over to his car, opened the trunk and put the envelope in the outside pocket of his suitcase. He was just a few discreet bank transactions away from the life he had always dreamed of.

Erik hit the gas, drove out of town, and never looked back.

CHAPTER EIGHT

Anne sat at her kitchen table and watched the procession of people as they filed across the footbridge and wound their way up the hill on her grandfather's island. Bryan had invited her to participate – something about being the matron of honor or the patron saint of oneness – but she didn't have the patience or the energy.

Safely alone, she sipped an iced tea garnished with peppermint and a splash of grapefruit juice, secure in knowing that this was the final event of the summer. Dr. Parsons had completed his initial underwater survey, and despite wanting to start excavations above ground, had agreed to wait until the following year. He had plenty of data to play with until then and was still madly trying to translate the glyphs on the stones and the markings on the cave walls.

It was almost over.

Through the window, Anne heard clapping, singing, and the occasional cheer from whatever was unfolding on the hill. She finished her tea and then busied herself with preparing dinner. She had some fresh whitefish in her oven that had spent the night in her fridge, soaking in a delicate cucumber-dill marinade she had learned from Gunther. Paired with a small salad tossed with an herb vinaigrette and a glass of Riesling, she would be a happy woman tonight.

From her perch at the kitchen table, she chopped some vegetables and watched the people streaming back the other direction. They were holding candles, some still burning, smiling and laughing. A couple of people broke free from the pack and started to walk toward the cottage, but were quickly tugged back into line by their friends. They were leaving her alone, just as Bryan had promised.

Bryan was the last person across the footbridge. His companion replaced the no trespassing sign and the two of them headed for her front door. Anne recognized Dylan immediately. His face had been etched on her brain for the past two days.

She sighed and went to the door to meet them.

"Hey, Annie," Bryan said and smiled. "I just wanted to say thanks. I hope I see you again next year."

"You're welcome, Bryan," Anne replied. "You always came through on your promises. Truth be told, you're the only person I trusted through all this."

"And I wanted to say I'm sorry," Dylan added, "for ignoring Bryan the other night and taking advantage of your trust." He held up a small grocery bag, filled with raspberries. "I picked these for you on the path leading up to the hill."

"Thank you," Anne said and took the bag. "I appreciate that, but it really wasn't necessary." She thought about the dinner cooking in her oven and devised a plan to stretch it into three portions. "Would the two of you like to join me for dinner?"

"I need to get back to camp and make sure everything wraps up according to plan," Bryan said, "but you two have fun." He winked and walked up the garden path to the main road.

Anne opened the door and stepped aside so Dylan could come into the cottage.

"Whatever that is, it smells great."

"Thanks," Anne said, "I was just about to take it out of the oven. Come on over to the table."

Dylan sat at the table while Anne finished preparing the meal. She got Dylan a glass, filled it with ice and then poured some tea. She put a handful of greenery onto her butcher block, chopped it up and put it into the glass, along with a splash of fruit juice. She gave it a stir and then set it on the table, along with the tossed salad and the whitefish.

Dylan waited politely for Anne to join him and then took a sip of the iced tea. He didn't know what it was, but it tasted familiar, and it wasn't just the drink – Anne's movements, the way she gathered the ingredients, the way she paused and looked up at him from what she was doing – the whole experience was remarkably familiar to Dylan.

"I'm not sure what happened the other night," he said, breaking the silence, "but I feel like I know you. I feel connected to you somehow, like I know everything about you." He looked at Anne for reassurance. "I feel like you know me too," he continued, "like we're old friends or something. How is that possible?"

"I don't know," Anne said, "but I know what you mean. I haven't been able to get your face out of my head the past few days. It's like I've known you my whole life."

Dylan smiled, relieved that Anne felt the same way, and he fought back the urge to blurt out everything that had been happening to him. He couldn't tell her everything. What was he supposed to say? That he had been talking to his dead wife in a box of light all summer and had seen little dead girls in the cemetery?

"I just don't know what is real," he said. "It's mostly images and feelings, but that's why I came to the hill the other night."

"What do you mean?" Anne asked taking a bite of her salad.

"When I was on the hill today, I felt things, I saw things," Dylan said. "It was very strange. Have you ever had funny feelings up there?"

"I've been going to the hill since I was a kid," Anne said. "My grandfather used to go up there with me. He's the one that taught me..." Anne hesitated, suddenly unsure of herself. She had never shared her spirituality with anyone before, not even Celeste. It was hers and hers alone, unsullied by other's opinions and prejudices.

Anne took a sip of her iced tea and looked into Dylan's emerald eyes. He was different than everyone else she had met this summer – authentic, kind – even without the odd connection they had felt outside her cottage, she trusted him.

"Taught you...?" Dylan asked in anticipation.

"Taught me how to respect nature," Anne continued, "how to get in touch with the seasons of the earth, the cycles of the moon – to find my balance, my center – and communicate with my guardian."

Anne paused and looked at Dylan across the kitchen table. She waited for him to break out laughing or say something degrading, but he just took another bite of his salad and chewed.

"Are you a spiritual person, Dylan?"

"If by spiritual, you mean religious, then not particularly, no," Dylan said. "I was raised Catholic, but Mary and I were always too busy living life to skip sleeping in and go sit on a hard bench every Sunday." He took a bite of fish. "Whoa, this is amazing."

"Thanks," Anne said, relieved by Dylan's nonchalance. "Mary?"

"My wife," Dylan said, filling his mouth with another bite.

"You're married?" Anne noticed the ring on Dylan's hand for the first time.

"She's dead," Dylan said out of the corner of his mouth. "She died about a year ago." He swallowed and took a drink. "She's buried over in Eagleton, in Lakeview Cemetery, just outside of town. She..." Dylan had never said this part out loud before, "...she killed herself."

"Oh," Anne said quietly, "I'm sorry."

"That's the main reason I'm here," Dylan decided to go for broke. "I've been having conversations with Mary lately, and she's the one who told me to come up here to the hill."

"Excuse me?" Anne said.

"I see dead people, Anne," Dylan said with a half-smile. "Apparently, it's one of my superpowers."

"You know," Anne said, trying to look unphased, "I've always wanted to talk to Abraham Lincoln. What do you say? Can you conjure him up for a quick chat?"

"It doesn't work like that," Dylan said.

"Oh, come on, I promise I'll be discreet."

"To be honest, I'm not really sure how I do it," Dylan said. "She – Mary – tends to find me, I just know where to look is all."

"Wait," Anne set down her fork, "you're serious? You see her? You see your dead wife and have real, actual conversations?"

"Yes," Dylan said, "what did you think I meant?"

"I don't know," Anne said, "I guess I thought you were talking metaphorically or something. I mean, I have conversations on the hill, so I can relate."

"Conversations?" Dylan asked.

"Yeah," Anne cleared her throat and looked down at her plate. "Sometimes I'll get a feeling or a subtle suggestion, maybe a word or phrase will pop into my mind while I'm meditating up there. Sometimes I hear voices. You know, that sort of thing."

Anne raised her eyes and Dylan nodded his head up and down.

"So, you're not throwing me out?" He asked. "After the whole shotgun thing, I was kind of afraid to share that with you. I have to ask, if I had started to walk up the hill to the stone circle, would you have shot me?"

"No," she replied, "shooting someone requires bullets, Dylan. The gun was just for effect, and no, I'm not kicking you out. In fact, I'm relieved too. I've never talked about that part of my life with anyone before."

Anne looked out the kitchen window at the darkening sky.

"Why don't you stay here tonight?" She asked, then quickly added, "on the couch."

"Thanks, that sounds a lot better than walking back across the island to sleep on the ground." Dylan smiled. "Look, I may not know everything about us and what's going on, but I promise you, I'm not here to hurt you."

"I know."

***

Anne shuffled up the hill, her feet like concrete blocks. A satchel weighed down her left shoulder as she struggled through the mist toward the ring of stones. She couldn't make out anything beyond what was right in front of her face, but she knew where she was going, and no matter how hard she tried, she couldn't stray from the path.

Anne stopped at what was left of the ring of stones, their crumbled remains a shadow of their former glory, the once proud Oak tree split into three parts and scattered on the ground. The center of the trunk had been hollowed out like a seat. This was her throne. She dropped the satchel in front of the tree and took her place on its splintered remains. Sharp needles poked and prodded at Anne's back and behind her knees as she waited for them to come.

First to arrive was her grandfather. He stopped at the altar and took a small part of it in his hands. He knelt in front of her, then placed the stone in Anne's satchel. "My promise to you," he said before walking away into the mist.

Next was Nancy, a look of sorrow and pain on her face. She stopped at the altar, just like her grandfather had, and took a piece in her hand. She knelt and placed the stone in Anne's satchel. "My promise to you," she said and walked away.

Anne watched as her nearest and dearest friends came up the path; Gunther, limping slowly, bones sticking out of the flesh of his broken leg; Celeste, her face broken and hair matted with blood.

"My promise to you," they said, dropping a piece of the altar into Anne's satchel and disappearing into the shadows.

Anne stood up as Dylan walked slowly up the path, the same look of pain and sorrow on his face. He stopped and kneeled at Anne's feet, his mouth parting, as if searching for words.

"What is it?" Anne asked. She reached for Dylan, but her arms were pinned unnaturally to her sides.

Dylan began coughing, and blood came pouring from his mouth. He reached for Anne in fear, unable to speak. Coughing again, Dylan's blood splattered across Anne's face and body before he fell face first to the ground next to the offering of rocks at her feet.

Her arms finally able to move, she knelt on the ground and cradled Dylan's head in her lap. "Dylan! What is it? Tell me..."

He looked up, gurgling and gasping for air before his body finally stopped moving.

Anne woke with a start, her heart still pounding from the dream. She walked out into the front room of the cottage and looked at Dylan, asleep on her couch. She knelt beside him, watching his chest rise and fall, and listened to the cadence of his breathing. Slowly, she began to calm down. As her pulse returned to normal, she closed her eyes and pictured herself in his arms. It was so familiar, like she had spent her entire life drifting off to sleep with her head on his chest, his breath on her cheek.

"Anne, what are you doing?" Dylan started to sit up.

"Shit!" Anne picked her head up from his chest and felt the warmth of her embarrassment creep into her face. "I'm sorry," she said, "I was just. I was just resting, and I...I didn't realize I was actually touching you."

"It's okay," Dylan smiled.

"I just had a terrible dream," she said, "about you and the hill. It ended with your head in my hands, just like the night we met."

"Yikes," Dylan replied, "I was just dreaming about ice cream."

"Come on, I'm serious," Anne said.

"So am I," Dylan replied. "Fried ice cream, with caramel sauce from Village Sweets down on Front Street in Eagleton."

"I've had dreams of the hill for as long as I can remember," Anne said. "I suppose I never made much of them because my grandfather lived here, but the hill and the stone circle have always been positive for me, Dylan. Since I met you, I've been getting horrible, violent images. Why is that?"

"I don't know," Dylan replied, "but I've had dreams about the hill before, too. They were about some sort of battle, so I guess they were violent, but that wasn't how they made me feel. I felt confident when I woke up, confident that I had to complete a task up there, and that it would be a good thing."

Dylan reached out to comfort Anne. As he put his hands in hers, familiar longings swept over him. He was so comfortable with her, yet she was new and perplexing all at the same time. A lock of Anne's peppery white hair was lying across her eye, and Dylan became transfixed.

"I really like your hair," he said. "The color."

"Oh," Anne smoothed the sides of her head, "thanks. I'm actually black by nature, but my hair started to go grey when I was still working, so I did this to even the score."

"Really?" He asked.

"Yeah," replied Anne. "Stress is a relentless little bitch, in my experience."

"Well, it suits you," Dylan replied.

He reached up and brushed the renegade lock of hair behind her ear, and voices began to echo in his head. They were faint at first, but they kept getting louder, like competing conversations at a dinner party, until one voice – Anne's voice – broke free from the chatter. She whispered sweetly to him and giggled. Images of Anne flashed across his mind, and her warm breath, smiling face and naked body flooded his head.

Anne took in a sharp breath and stood up.

"Did you feel that just now?" she asked.

"Yeah," Dylan replied, "it was like the other day, wasn't it?"

"I was with you. You were. We were," Anne gestured with her hands.

"Naked," Dylan finished her thought. "We were somewhere safe and warm, but I couldn't make out exactly where. It felt like home."

Dylan looked at Anne for reassurance.

"There was a fireplace," Anne finished his thought, "a huge hearth with a roaring fire. Something was cooking. It smelled so good. You looked so good."

Anne stopped, suddenly embarrassed.

"It's okay," Dylan said, standing up. "I know. I felt it too."

"Do you have any idea what's going on?" Anne asked.

"Not exactly," Dylan replied, "I've never felt like this before, but it's so familiar at the same time. Does that make sense?"

"Yes," she replied. "I didn't know you existed until a few days ago, but I feel like I know every intimate detail about you." She looked down at his waist where her gaze lingered until she felt the heat surge back into her cheeks. "But just the same," she returned her gaze to his eyes, "I don't feel attracted to you...sexually, I just mean...connected."

"Yeah, I know what you mean," Dylan said. "Not that I don't find you attractive, it's just—"

"Yeah, no, I mean, obviously I think you're good looking and all that, but..." Anne bit her lip. "Are you hungry?"

"I could eat a horse," Dylan said. "After we eat, can we go to the hill? Maybe it will help us get things sorted?"

"I'd like that."

CHAPTER NINE

As Anne and Dylan came up the path and the rocks came into view, images raced through his mind, familiar, but distant.

"I could swear I've been here before," Dylan said. "I've seen the hill in my dreams, just like you." He stepped to the side of the stone circle, toward the large oak tree that towered over them.

Anne walked over to where Dylan stood.

"There," she said, pointing to the ground under the oak. "That's where you were when I was holding your head in my hands. Whatever we were doing up here, something went wrong, I can feel it. It's like a tingling through my whole body."

"You're tingling too?" Dylan said and walked over to the tree. "I'm pretty sure you're right. Something happened up here that we couldn't finish. It feels like it was us, but that's impossible." Dylan looked around on the ground and up at the stones. "Something's missing." He closed his eyes and tried to remember his dreams. "There was a bright white rock over there in that stone." Dylan walked over and reached up, running his hand over a depression in one of the stones. "It sat right in here, and it was glowing white."

"I remember!" Anne said. "Yes! It was sending white light down into the ground, toward the cave, and out into the circle of stones. But, why? What were we doing?" She walked into the center of the hill and looked up. She gave Dylan a coy smile and held out her hands. "Come here, Dylan, come here and hold my hands."

Dylan took Anne by the hands.

"Oh...shit," she gasped.

Anne wasn't prepared for the intense sensation that started in her fingers, radiated up her arms, then rippled down her spine and tickled her toes. She could feel the warmth of Dylan's touch all over her body. She quickly broke free from his grasp.

"Tell me you felt that," she said, stepping backward away from him.

"Don't you see me shaking over here?" Dylan replied. "There must be something to this, and that means…" Dylan paused.

"What?" Anne asked.

"It means I haven't been losing my mind," Dylan said, "that those things really happened to me, and that Mary was right – we're supposed to do something up here."

"What things, Dylan?"

"I don't have a fucking clue," Dylan said.

"Dy-lan!" The familiar mocking tone of Mary's voice came out of the trees around them. "Here, Dyly-Dyly!"

"Hey!" Anne shouted at Mary as she emerged from the forest. "The party's over, so get lost!"

"What's the matter, Dylan? Haven't you told her about us?" Mary snickered and walked toward them. "He comes to visit me all the time in the cemetery, but I have to say, I really don't approve of all his girlfriends."

Mary gave Anne a narrow glance.

"What's going on," Anne asked Dylan. "Who is this?"

"You need to leave," Dylan said to Mary. "You don't belong here."

"Don't belong here? Really, Dylan?" Mary said, circling around them. "Do you two think you can get away with this? You can't possibly finish what was started here."

"Dylan, what's going on?" Anne asked. "I mean it," she said to Mary, "you need to turn around, walk down the hill, and go back to the camp with everyone else."

Mary cocked her head to one side and smiled, then dropped to all fours on the path, convulsing and shaking her head from side to side. Anne gasped as Mary's body began to stretch and grow, creaked like a falling tree and then imploded into a whirling black mass. An ear-wrenching shriek pierced the darkness of the forest as the cyclone slowly dissipated and then melted into a fine black mist.

"Fuck," Dylan said and looked nervously at Anne.

The black fog whirled around Dylan and Anne, surrounding them and expanding until it covered the stone circle and the entire hill. Muted groans came out of the darkness from all directions, and the air buzzed with frenzied whispers.

"Wha—what are you?" Anne stuttered.

"*What* am I?" A deep voice retorted from the shadows. "The arrogance of your species never fails to amuse me." A rush of icy-cold air passed between Anne and Dylan, leaving a surge of raw heat in its wake that made them both stumble backwards. "You aren't capable of speaking my name, you miserable wretch, but I'm here because you're mine."

Anne spun around in the darkness, desperately looking for a way out. The mist enveloped the entire hill, and even though it was nearly midday, she could barely see from one end of the stone circle to the other.

"Dylan!" Her words seemed to bounce back into her face as soon as they left her mouth, and then echoed wildly in all directions. She held out her hands and spun around looking for him.

"I'm here!" came his cacophonous reply.

Dylan's hands found hers, and she was instantly comforted. The warmth of his touch – even the fear in his eyes – let her know that she wasn't alone.

"And what about you, Anne Leahy," the deep voice bellowed, "do you know what you really are?"

Anne stared blankly at the question. She had no idea what that meant, but she wasn't about to back down. Not here. Not on her grandfather's hill. She took a deep breath, let go of Dylan's hands, and took a defiant step forward.

"Anne?" Dylan looked to her for reassurance, but she was already scanning the unnatural fog that surrounded them.

In a single, swift motion, the beast closed on its prey. Anne's body stiffened as a whirling black cloud gathered around her neck. She clawed at her throat and kicked frantically as her feet left the ground.

"You really don't know, do you?" It laughed as she struggled to breathe. "You're fodder, like all the rest."

It released its grip and Anne fell to the ground, gasping and choking as she got back to her knees. Dylan reached Anne's side and the reaper's grip found his throat instead. The air rippled and the dark whispers that echoed through the mist turned to anxious shouts.

"How can you be so whole after what I did to you?"

A bright white heat came out of Dylan's chest, pulsing slowly at first, and then faster as the whirling black mass and Dylan began to shake violently in rhythm together. Dylan felt like every cell in his body was simultaneously ignited, burning him alive from the inside out. He screamed in agony as the pain tore through him.

"Dylan!"

Anne tackled him by the waist, wrenching him free from the scorching heat of the dark embrace. She fell to the ground with Dylan's limp body and covered it defensively. She could hear the voices again, surrounding her and Dylan in a counterpoint of nervous chatter and uneasy laughter.

"You can't have him!" Anne screamed and got to her feet.

She felt an instinct growing inside of her, like a tingling that began in her toes and hummed all through her body. This was a rage she had never felt before, a raw power aching for release. She took a step forward, and a ripple cut through the dark cloud, a wave of light that cut through the darkness and out beyond the hill. For the first time since the encounter began, Anne saw the sun reflecting off the rich blue waters of Lake Huron.

"I said leave!" Anne shouted.

The mist swirled around Anne again, enveloping her face and clamping down around her shoulders. She fell to her knees, gasping for air. Anne's chest was just beginning to scorch in a blinding flash of white light when another blur of black motion broke her free and knocked her to the ground next to Dylan.

Dylan coughed and stirred.

"Fucking hell," he managed and took a deep breath.

"Are you okay?" She asked, choking.

"I think so," Dylan replied. "My chest is killing me, but I think so. You?"

"Same," Anne said and rubbed her shoulder.

Across the stone circle at the edge of the clearing, the frenzied voices got louder, until they became a single, agonizing shriek.

"You," the voice of the first reaper ripped through the mist of the hill. "They belong to me."

There was no reply, but as its whirling mass fully extended, it became obvious that the second reaper was larger and more powerful than the first. The voices emanating from it were louder, more distinct, but still unintelligible to Anne and Dylan. The smaller demon bolted around the hill, a ball of black mist, frantically trying to escape. Each time it reached the edge of the circle, a deep thud would send it shrieking in another direction.

"Come on," Anne said, leading Dylan to a safer perch, just behind the oak tree.

The struggle between the two reapers didn't last much longer. The boundaries of the first reaper's prison got steadily smaller, and it raced back and forth, until it had nowhere to go. It hovered at the center of the hill, spinning wildly in a tight circle, and then let out a piercing scream. Anne tried to cover her ears, but her hands moved slowly, and then stopped altogether. It was like all the motion and sound had been sucked out of the hill. A moment later, the dark swirling mass exploded in a hail of sparkling black confetti, and the battle was over. Time began to flow again, and Anne took a deep breath.

"You can come out now," a voice rumbled. "I'm not here to hurt you."

Dylan and Anne walked out from behind the oak tree and into the stone circle.

The whirling black cloud seemed to fold back in on itself, changing – in the blink of an eye – into human form. Where the whirling black cloud of voices and nightmares had been, a young woman with black dreadlocks now stood. Her lips and face were painted with dark crimson war paint, accentuating her black eyes. The paint continued down her thick, muscular torso, a series of circular patterns that wrapped around her hips and were clearly visible behind the translucent surface of her skintight black armor. Two shimmering swords were strapped to her back.

"Your mouth is open," Anne said to Dylan, throwing an elbow.

"What...who are you?" Dylan asked, scanning awkwardly for a spot where his eyes wouldn't bask in the alluring lethalness of the woman in the center of the stone circle.

"Your kind used to call me Aislinn," she said in a husky, feminine tone. As the remnants of the black cloud dissipated, the hill was again bathed in sunlight. "But that was thousands of years ago."

"Pfft," Dylan scoffed sarcastically.

"What do you know about time, Dylan Ward?" Aislinn asked.

"Wait, how do you know my name?"

"Because, I've been watching you," she said, and looked at Anne. "Both of you."

"Alright," Anne said, "so, why are you here, and why are you helping us?"

"I've been waiting for you," Aislinn said. "I've watched tens of thousands of your ancestors be born, live and die, waiting for you to come here together to this place."

"You knew this would happen?" Dylan asked. "Can you travel through time or something?"

"Time only has one direction," Aislinn said, "but many speeds. It can't be stopped, but it can be warped, twisted and slowed. Your planet was cursed by the darkness millennia ago, and now you creep on at a snail's pace, blissfully ignorant of your fate, and feeding the darkness in other planes."

"I don't follow." Dylan gestured at the stone circle. "So, why are you helping us?"

"I wish it had always been so," Aislinn said, "but I was born to the darkness, spawned by the void. I served it willingly – like countless others – for," she stopped and smiled at Dylan, "*thousands* of years."

Dylan smiled back, desperately trying to maintain eye contact.

"Our sole purpose," Aislinn said and jumped onto one of the nearby stones, "was to hunt down every trace of the light, the energy that lives inside of you." In a single blur of motion, Aislinn backflipped onto the ground, drew the swords from her back, and crossed their shimmering blades against Dylan's throat. "To destroy you," she giggled, "and feed you to the darkness."

"Yeah, cool," Dylan slowly stepped clear of her blades. "Okay."

"But here," she lifted her swords to the sky, "a resistance started."

Aislinn got into a battle stance and went through a series of graceful, acrobatic movements with her blades, before sheathing them. "But it was too late. Without the knowledge of your gift, you – and your planet – became irrelevant. People like you and Anne survived in small groups, taken for sport by my former dark comrades." She moved to where Anne was standing. "But even as your kind teetered on the brink of extinction, I continued to question your fate. I knew that one day, someone would come along to restore this plane, to take it back from the darkness."

"How are we supposed to do that?" Anne asked.

"Does it have something to do with this hill?" Dylan added.

"Yes," Aislinn responded, "but I don't know how they did it, or why these stones are important. All I know is, the two of you are the key."

"I don't get it," Dylan said. "I don't understand how all of our modern science has missed something like an epic worldwide battle that raged on for centuries. Kind of a big deal to have it just slip on by undetected, don't you think?"

"Wait, Dylan," Anne leaned against the nearest stone. "Maybe we have. This darkness," she said to Aislinn, "are we talking about a black hole?"

"I don't know what that means," Aislinn replied.

"A black hole is an area of intense gravity," Anne explained. "So intense that not even light can escape it. If you were to fall into a black hole, time would seem to pass normally, but to an outside observer, it would be so slow, it would appear to stand still."

"Precisely," Aislinn said.

"We think that every galaxy has a super massive black hole at its center," Anne continued, "feeding on the energy of nearby stars."

"Fucking hell," Dylan chirped.

"But that's not all," Anne said, staring absently at the horizon. "There's this stuff called dark matter that they haven't even figured out yet. Like some sort of cosmic glue that makes up 95 percent of everything."

"What?" Dylan asked incredulously.

"Their words, Dylan, not mine." Anne said.

Aislinn looked up to the sky.

"I've secured this hill, for now," she said, "but my presence here will attract others."

She leaned in and kissed the center of Anne's forehead, and a soothing warmth pulsed down Anne's spine. It moved slowly forward into her abdomen and then centered on her chest, just above her heart. Aislinn traced a gentle path down Anne's cheek and across her shoulder with her fingertips, then placed the palm of her hand on Anne's chest and began to massage it in small, tight circles.

"Just because something is forgotten, doesn't mean it's lost forever. Now that you've found each other, you need to stay together." Aislinn motioned for Dylan to come closer, and a brilliant white light enveloped the hill. “You’re stronger together.”

Anne turned to Dylan, took him by the hand, and he was bathed in the warmth that now surged through both of their bodies. As the light hummed around them, Anne wrapped her arms around his waist and buried her head in his shoulder while he held her close. It wasn’t until the warmth of their embrace faded, and the light disappeared, that they realized they were alone.

“Shit,” Anne said and took a few steps back.

“You’re fine,” Dylan said, “I wanted you to – I mean – you’re good. It’s good.”

He exhaled.

“You know,” he shook his hands and rubbed his chest, “when that thing attacked, I felt like I was on fire, but now,” he looked into Anne’s eyes, “now, I feel invincible! My whole body is tingling again, just like when we got up here. Do you feel it?”

Oh, she felt it. Whatever was causing their connection, being here on the hill with Dylan was doing wonders for Anne’s confidence, and it surged right along with the energy buzzing in her chest. Without thinking, she closed the distance between them, moving so quickly that she tripped, and caused an awkward collision that nearly spoiled the whole moment. Her chin collided with Dylan’s shoulder and he had to grab her with both arms to break her fall. She didn’t say anything – she didn’t try to apologize or explain it away – she just made her move.

Dylan responded immediately to the warm sweetness of her lips and tongue, pulled her close and kissed her deeply. As the moments passed, Anne sensed a more familiar energy. The healing energy of the hill that she had learned to harness surrounded them both, covering them like a warm blanket on a cold night.

Anne broke off their embrace with a series of gentle caresses on his cheek and neck, then buried her head under Dylan’s chin.

“Sorry,” she said.

"Really?"

"No."

"Good."

"I might have lied back in the cabin," Anne said. "I'm totally attracted to you."

"Fair enough," Dylan replied. "Me, too."

"There's something about us, this light – our energy – that just seems so perfect." Anne said.

As the adrenaline of their embrace faded, reality crept in. A shapeshifting demon had just tried to devour her soul, and then she kissed a man she had known for less than 24 hours. Anne felt a wave of nausea ripple through her stomach, and her hands began to tremble. She sat down, leaned against the trunk of the oak tree and rubbed her temples.

"You sure you're alright?" Dylan asked.

"I'm fine," Anne said, "it's just sinking in, I guess. Without Aislinn, we'd be dead right now."

"Yeah, I know," Dylan replied. "The first time that reaper attacked me, it scared me so bad that I..."

"What?" Anne prompted.

"Nothing," Dylan said, then quickly said. "Abigail chased it off for me with some sort of superpower, and she said that I – that we – have it, too. You did something up here, though. I saw you do it. It was like some wave of energy came out of your body and it slowed the reaper down. How did you do that, anyway?"

"I have no clue," Anne replied. "Wait, who's Abigail?"

"I don't know, exactly," Dylan replied, "but she said that we're the light of the stars, or something like that. I'm sure she could help us."

"Where does she live?"

"Lakeview Cemetery."

"She's dead, too?"

"Yeah, and so are her kids."

"Seriously, what the fuck?" Anne shook her head. She'd had enough supernatural for one day, thank you very much. "Well, if we need to find out more about the hill and what happened up here, there's only one place I know with the answers."

"The cemetery?" Dylan asked, thinking of Abigail.

"No, the library," Anne said.

CHAPTER TEN

When the ferry snugged into the dock in Eagleton, Dylan and Anne disembarked and fought their way through the crowd at the ticket station. The dock was filled with cars and clogged with pedestrians trying to catch the next ferry to the island. The crowd thinned out as they got away from the dock and they followed the sidewalk on the edge of the water into town. It was mid-morning, but the row of buildings across from the water already had a palpable energy.

They turned up the main road leading into town and walked two blocks up the hill to the library, which doubled as a local history museum. Dylan held open the door for Anne and then followed behind. A man in his late twenties was behind the counter, staring at a computer screen. His bushy beard and ponytail seemed out of kilter with the refined look of his khaki pants and navy-blue cardigan. Dylan was about to say hello when the man looked at Anne and his eyes got wide.

"Hey, aren't you –"

"Do yourself a favor and don't say it," Dylan interrupted. "I'm hoping to find some information on people who lived around here back in the 1800s."

The young man looked past Dylan and smiled.

"I'm Dale," he said, rosy-cheeked.

"Hi, Dale! It's great to meet you, buddy!" Dylan said and waved his hand back and forth in front of his face. "About those dead people?"

"Sure, no problem," he said with a smirk.

Dylan couldn't resist.

"And Lady Leahy wanted to learn more about the rocks on top of her hill," he said. "That is, if you don't mind helping her."

Dylan saw Anne's right hand flex into the shape of a fist.

"Of course!" Dale said. Dylan couldn't be sure, but he thought the young man's hands were actually shaking. "Follow me and I'll get you started. Place is pretty empty today, so I could give you a guided tour of our exhibit." He looked at Anne expectantly and floated around the counter. "I'm surprised we haven't had more people in here this summer, to be honest. I guess most people don't really care about the truth."

Dylan and Anne followed him over to a computer terminal and he gestured to Dylan to sit down.

"Alright, we're part of the Family World online knowledge network. This is the quickest way to find someone that lived here." He clicked the mouse and pointed at the screen. "Click 'new search' then put in the first and last name, then 'Eagleton' as the city. Let's do you as an example."

Dylan typed in his name and date of birth with his index fingers.

"Perfect, now, since you haven't been dead for 60 years, it would help if we knew the same for your parents."

Dylan obliged.

"Alright, now just click here and we'll see what comes up."

Dylan watched as names and boxes branched out like a web. There was so much information on the screen, it was too small to read.

"Wow, pretty cool, Dylan," Dale said.

"How's that?" Dylan asked.

"Well, it traced you all the way back to England in the 1400s, which is about as far as written records can take you. Sometimes other people link their research and family trees into the database. They've basically done all the work for you, lucky dog."

"My whole family tree is out there on the internet?" Dylan asked.

"Yep," Dale said. "You'd be surprised what people can do in their spare time. In this case, I'm not surprised. See this?" Dale pointed at a picture in the top left of the screen next to a username and email address. "That's Nancy McCoy."

"You know Nancy?" Anne asked.

"Yeah – well, I've met her a couple times – she comes to our annual fundraiser every summer. She's always been a generous supporter of the library and has a real passion for the local history collection. Ooh," Dale waved his hands with fake theatrics. "Looks like your people are from Salem, Dylan. You some kind of witch?"

"Salem." Dylan squinted at the screen. "Really?"

"Yep," Dale said. "Look, right here," he said and pointed. "Usually, we charge 10 cents a page, but I'll print this off for you for free since you're a friend of Miss Leahy."

He looked at Anne and smiled.

She didn't smile back.

Dale clicked the mouse and the printer behind the counter whirred to life.

"So, what's the name of the person you are hoping to learn more about?" Dale asked.

"Abigail," Dylan replied, "but I don't know her last name. I do know when she died, though."

"Who's Abigail?" Anne asked.

"I'll tell you later," Dylan said, "assuming I can find her in this machine."

"Right," Dale said. "I'll leave you to it, Dylan. Let me know if you have any questions." He turned to Anne and held out his arm. "The exhibit is over this way."

Dylan started pecking at the keyboard again and Anne followed Dale into the next room. There were three display cases, overflowing with everyday items and other assorted sundries. Next to them, a large red lumber cart with two enormous wheels sat at an angle. Dale kept a respectful distance and let Anne take it all in.

"This is just about a lumber company," she said, pointing at a picture in the case, "and that man. Who is he?"

"Well, to be honest," Dale looked into the case, "until that video of yours, this was all we knew about the hill."

The video isn't mine, Anne thought, picturing Erik Larson trapped under a rock on the bottom of Lake Huron, running out of air.

"It's Hyram Dunning."

"Nancy McCoy's great-grandfather?"

"Well, yes, actually," Dale's smile got even bigger. "It's so nice to have visitors who know what they're talking about. As I'm sure *you* know, Dunning had a lumber company. He owned most of the county back in the pioneer days, pretty typical stuff. He cut down all the trees and when the timber ran out, he sold the land to farmers."

Anne scanned the case and her eyes locked on a piece of wood with a symbol burned into it.

"What's that?"

"That's the brand for the Dunning Lumber Company," Dale said. "Hasn't been any press about it, but yes, it's one of the symbols they found on your hill. I figure some YouTuber looking for a unique spin will be waltzing through the front door any day now." He looked over his shoulder, then back at Anne. "At any rate, he used to own your island, too. I figure he came across the symbol and thought it would be unique. They used to burn their brand into their lumber, kind of like cattle, so they could identify it at the mill."

Anne scanned the case and then looked at the symbol again. A low hum began in her ear, and her eyebrow began to twitch.

"His story really is extraordinary," Dale continued. "It demonstrates the power of conviction, determination, and the American spirit of progress."

"Really," Anne said with fake interest, a conversational skill she had perfected these past few months. "How so?"

"His wife Abigail and two daughters died in an accident up on the hill," Dale said.

"Accident?" Anne said, genuinely interested.

"Yeah," Dale said, "nobody knows exactly what happened, but they found all three of them dead on the rocks at the base of the hill. Personally, I think they went Grand Canyon."

"Grand Canyon?"

"Yeah, I figure the little girls were playing too close to the edge of the hill and when they went over," he motioned down with his hands, "mom panicked and followed after."

"How awful," Anne said.

"I know," Dale replied, "but it was that tragedy that catapulted Hyram's vision for Pine Island and Eagleton forward. Kind of inspiring, actually."

"Unless you were Native American, or liked trees." Anne retorted.

"Yes, well, I suppose, but – "

"So, Dale, is there anything else that isn't on display?" Anne rubbed her spastic eyebrow and then tucked a few wisps of hair behind her ears. "You know," she reached out and gently touched his shoulder, "for famous people like me?"

His cheeks flushed and he looked around the empty room.

"There are a few boxes in the archives," he said, "but they're not really top-secret or anything. To be honest, I was already going to show you. Would you like to see them now?"

Anne smiled and nodded her head.

He took an ID badge out of his pocket, waved it in front of a nearby door and then waited for Anne to enter the hallway where another keypad waited next to a large door. The musty smell that rushed out of the room took Anne by surprise. Even for a museum it was rank. The shelves were overflowing with papers, boxes and artifacts that only someone like Dr. Parsons could truly appreciate. Dale led Anne through the stacks, pulled two boxes off the shelves and set them on a stainless-steel table next to a window.

"These boxes have a few of Hyram Dunning's personal things. They've been part of the exhibits as they change over the years, but we keep them in here when they're not on display. I just need you to put on some gloves." Dale handed her some latex gloves from a box on the table and then looked at the door. "I really need to be at the desk, so I'm going to leave you here, if that's okay?"

"Sure," Anne said.

Dale shut the door behind him, and Anne was alone. She removed the lid from the first box and sighed. It looked like the wall of a Cracker Barrel restaurant. You could trade out anything from the case for what she saw in the box and nobody would know the difference. She replaced the lid and pushed the box aside.

The contents of the second box looked similar, but as Anne picked through the knick-knacks, her eyebrow began to twitch again. Underneath a ledger, there was a leather necklace with stone beads. As Anne's hand passed over the necklace, it glowed white, and when she pulled back her hand in surprise, the stones went dark. She poked at the necklace tentatively, expecting the stones to give her a shock. She looked over her shoulder at the closed door behind her, then picked it up. When she ran her fingers across the stones, they began to shimmer again, and she saw what they were.

Anne shoved the necklace in her pocket, slammed the lid on the box and walked quickly out of the room. Dylan stood near the front desk, pacing back and forth. When he saw Anne, he waved the stack of papers and gave her an anxious look.

"We need to talk," they both said at the same time.

Dylan held the door for Anne but couldn't hold back his excitement. He started talking before the door even closed behind her.

"Abigail's last name was Dunning," he said. "She was married to that lumber guy, Hyram!"

"Oh, that's the same Abigail that Dale told me about," she replied. "Isn't it horrible how she and her daughters died?"

"I know, I read about in this article I found on the computer. It was written after Hyram died," Dylan said and held up the papers he had printed out. "It says that 'despite being grief-stricken and prone to fits of rage, he continued to run Dunning Lumber and Shipping with an iron fist for another forty years until his death in 1885 from a bout with pneumonia.'"

"Why are you interested in Abigail, anyway?" Anne asked.

"Not here," Dylan said and pointed at all the people on the sidewalk. "But check this out – she and I have a common ancestor back in England. And look!" Dylan traced a line through the generations with his index finger. "It's the same line that ended up in Salem."

"Small world," Anne said. She looked over her shoulder at the museum door and tugged at Dylan's arm. "Come on, let's get out of here," she said. "I need to show you something, too."

She led him down the street toward the bay. Families were clogging the streets, and there was a line for the ice cream shop that spilled out onto the sidewalk. When they got to the water, she turned up Front Street and they got lost in the throngs of tourists before ducking into Chauncey's Leather Goods & Book Emporium. A neon yellow sign in the shape of an explosion read *'t-shirts, $15.'*

Dylan had never seen or smelled so much leather in his life. He had no idea so many things were made from it, or that they could all fit into one tiny store. Place mats, coasters, clothing, dream catchers, journals, portfolios, pet collars, keychains and bookmarks – an entire case of bookmarks – filled one-half of the shop from floor to ceiling. The other half was filled with new and used books of every genre and persuasion.

And t-shirts.

"Hey, Chauncey," Anne said to the middle-aged man with thick, black glasses behind the counter. "How are you?"

"Well, look who it is," he replied, looking up from his book "I'm well, thanks. I haven't seen you yet this summer."

"Yeah..." Anne drew the word out and wrinkled her nose, "been a little busy."

"So, I've heard. Let me know if you need any help."

He looked at Dylan.

"Oh, right – this is my friend Dylan. Dylan, Chauncey."

"Nice to meet you, Dylan," he said and resumed his reading.

Anne walked down an aisle of books and motioned Dylan to follow.

"Check this out," she said. "It was in with Hyram Dunning's stuff." She took the amulet out of her pocket and held it up by its leather chain.

"Whoa," Dylan said, "you stole it?" He looked over his shoulder and continued in a whisper. "You stole that from the library?"

"Yeah, but here's why," Anne replied softly. She slowly passed her finger across the stones allowing each one to light up one by one. Dylan's eyes got wide.

"Those are the markings from the stones on the hill!" He shouted.

"I know," Anne put her finger to her lips and then put the amulet back into her pocket. "I wish we knew what Hyram found on the hill and why he had this necklace."

"He's buried in Lakeview Cemetery, right?"

Anne nodded.

"Maybe we can go talk to him," Dylan said.

Anne blinked.

"My superpower, remember?" Dylan said. "I might be able to talk to him and find out what he knows."

Talking to a corpse was not on Anne's bucket list, and the thought of meeting Hyram Dunning for a chat was more than unnerving. "I don't know," she said, and started pacing back and forth.

"Everything alright?" Chauncey called from his perch.

"Yeah, hey, Chauncey – what would you recommend in the way of mindless summer romance? You know, the kind that borders on inappropriate, but is still considered socially acceptable?" Anne scratched her temple and tried to look like she was browsing.

"You can literally close your eyes and pick anything on the shelf behind you," he replied. "I guarantee, they'll all deliver."

"Got it," Anne said and picked one with a gaudy pink cover begging for attention. She grabbed a small leather pouch and placed both items on the counter. Dylan looked at the book, looked at Anne, looked at the book again and raised an eyebrow.

"What?" she said. "Like you've never met someone with an erotica habit before. Chauncey here is my dealer, of sorts."

"So, you want to hear today's 50% off music trivia challenge?" Chauncey asked.

"You know I do," Anne replied with a smile.

"Alright," Chauncey said, "which 80's pop singer was also a talented traditional Mexican folk singer and won a Grammy for best Mexican-American performance?"

"Uh...Pat Benetar?"

"Good guess, but no. Dylan?"

"Madonna?"

Chauncey sighed and looked at Anne.

"Linda Ronstadt," he said, "but since it's you, and you're almost as famous as she is now, I'll still give you the discount."

"Thanks, but you're only famous if you act like it." Anne said and put a twenty-dollar bill on the counter. "Keep the change."

She put the amulet into the leather pouch and put it back in her pocket.

"Look," she said to Dylan as they hit the sidewalk outside, "I want to believe you when you say that you see dead people, and after what happened on the hill, I'm sure you're not lying." She stopped and stepped aside for a couple pushing a stroller. "But what makes you think that we can just waltz into the cemetery and talk to Hyram Dunning?"

"Call it a hunch," Dylan replied. "His wife and children had – have – special powers and I doubt that was a secret."

"You think he has them too?" Anne asked.

"Let's go find out."

CHAPTER ELEVEN

It was after dark when they got to the cemetery. The heat of the day was gone, but the humidity still lay over them like a scratchy, wool blanket. Anne looked at the rows of tombstones on the other side of the fence. Her stomach was in knots – like someone was ringing out a wet towel – and her blood coursed with adrenaline.

"Are you sure this is a good idea?"

"It's fine," Dylan replied. "I come here all the time."

"Right, and talk to dead people." Anne shook her hands. "Don't you feel that?"

"Feel what?"

"I don't know," Anne said, wiping a bead of sweat from her eyebrow. "It's something in my gut. Literally. It just doesn't feel right."

"Come on," Dylan said, "it'll be fine." He bent down on one knee and cupped his hands. "Now that Aislinn took care of that other reaper, we shouldn't have anything to worry about."

With a final nervous glance up and down the street, Anne stepped into his hands, grabbed the top of the fence, and struggled over, landing on the ground with a grunt.

"Ouch! Shit, that hurt!"

Dylan quickly scaled the fence and joined her on the other side.

"See?" He said and helped her stand up. "No sweat."

Anne rubbed at her tailbone as they walked away from the fence.

"In case you hadn't noticed, the term *'skinny bitch'* was not invented to describe me."

"Rightly so," Dylan replied.

"Excuse me?" Anne said defensively. "What's that supposed to mean?"

"It means," Dylan replied, "that I really like how you're just – well – you're just you. I feel like I've known you forever, and I can't imagine you any other way. Trust me, I wouldn't hang out with someone forever if they were fake or always worried about what other people thought."

"Oh," Anne said, relaxing.

She was really starting to like Dylan Ward.

"Well, Body Mass Index aside, I'm still no angel," she said. "I spent the last 15 years trying to have more than everyone else."

"More of what?"

"Everything," Anne said with a frown.

"And how'd that go?" Dylan asked.

"Not so well," replied Anne with a wink, "for people who got in my way."

"So, now that you've seen the error of your ways, how are things shaping up?"

"Not bad," Anne said. She hooked her arm in his and hugged his shoulder. "But my new friend is a little dark. He likes to hang out in cemeteries at night." She looked at him and smiled. "Kind of creepy."

"Wait," Dylan said in mock horror. "Are you saying we're just friends? I've seen you naked!"

"Oh, stop."

The queasy feeling in Anne's stomach was almost gone. Being with Dylan – especially touching him – grounded her and put her at ease. Dylan felt it too. He hadn't been back to the cemetery since Mary attacked him. Even if he didn't want to admit it, he was nervous too, but being with Anne made him feel stronger. Instead of scanning for movement in the shadows, he laced his fingers on top of Anne's, and walked calmly down the path.

"Ah, the cemetery at night," Anne took a deep breath through her nose as they walked past the Union soldier. "I bet this is where you take all the girls."

"Actually, I was never here before Mary died," Dylan said.

"Oh, right," Anne said, suddenly embarrassed by her callousness. "Where is she buried?"

"Just over there, by the willow tree."

Through the mist, Anne could see the limbs of the tree arcing gracefully to the ground.

"What a beautiful tree," she said. "Can we stop there on the way?"

"Sure," he said and led her through the tombstones.

"It's really quite peaceful here," Anne said as they arrived at Mary's grave, "and I have to say, I think Mary has one of the best seats in the house."

Dylan knelt in front of Mary's grave.

"It's funny," he said and looked up at the sky, "but everything feels different somehow. Now that I know that she's out there somewhere, I don't feel quite as connected to her here."

"That's kind of the whole point, isn't it?" Anne said. She was walking in a circle around the trunk of the tree, touching the hanging limbs with outstretched arms. "She's moved on, and this is just a place for her remains to return to the earth. You know, the whole circle of life thing?"

"I guess," Dylan said.

Anne could tell that Dylan was still struggling, and she was reminded of a spell she had learned as a little girl. She took one of the willow branches in her hand and tied it in a knot, then looked up at the moon, a hazy half-circle filtering through the mist. *Please help my new friend finish healing,* she whispered and then blew a gentle kiss across the knotted branch.

She walked over and took Dylan's hand.

"Come on," she said, "let's get this over with."

When they got to the mausoleum, Dylan tried to open the door.

"Seriously?" Anne said.

"It was worth trying," Dylan said and picked up a large rock from the landscaping that surrounded the stone building. He took the rock with both hands and struck the door handle. Old and neglected, a few well-placed strikes left the latch rattling in the door frame. He pushed on the door and it gave slightly.

Dylan was about to put his shoulder into it when he heard something. Someone moaned on the other side of the door, and the sound of rattling chains echoed inside the building. The knot surged back into Anne's stomach and a rush of rank air washed over her face. It was smoky, but sharp – like vinegar – and her eyes began to water.

"Dylan, wait," she said. "I have a terrible feeling about this. Something very bad is in there. Something evil." Anne took two steps backwards. The knot in her gut intensified, like a swarm of agitated bees crawling under her skin. "Can't you feel that?"

"No," Dylan said and grabbed Anne by the arm. "Now, come on. If you want to talk to Hyram Dunning, he's – well – I think he's literally on the other side of this door."

Dylan didn't wait for Anne to reply. He threw his weight against the door and burst inside.

Hyram Dunning's emaciated body was chained to the far wall, his arms and legs secured separately, with just enough slack to allow him to move. A cast iron belt was fastened to his hips, with a large chunk of granite secured to his iron belt by another chain attached to his groin. He shuffled back and forth along the wall, dragging the block of stone between his legs.

"No, no, no," he moaned, until the chains on his legs went taught, then he turned and went back the other direction.

Dylan could see where his bare feet and the stone had worn a smooth path in the slab floor next to the wall. He was about to say hello when Anne stepped through the door. As soon as she was in the room, Hyram lunged his wiry frame at her, straining against the chains with his hands outstretched. He shrieked and his face contorted, shaking violently from side to side.

Dylan put himself between Anne and Hyram and held up his hands.

"Hey!" He shouted. "We're friends!"

Anne slapped Dylan's shoulder with the back of her hand. *Friends?* She mouthed cynically and shook her head.

Dylan looked Hyram in the eyes and his face began to relax, his rage turning to a simmer before it completely disappeared. He grabbed his bald head with both hands and retreated, then resumed his shuffling gate against the wall.

Dylan motioned to Anne, and she walked tentatively into the room. Seeing Hyram Dunning's living, breathing corpse chained to the wall, the fear she felt outside was confirmed. A dark cloud surrounded him, and when Anne looked in his eyes she saw nothing but a terrible, black void.

"Let's try that again," Dylan said. "Why are you chained to the wall, Mr. Dunning?"

"Crimes," he said, dragging the stone across the floor and taking a few more steps.

"What crimes?" Anne asked.

"I didn't know," he whimpered. "How could I know?" He stopped suddenly and looked at Dylan and Anne. "Two together, the two together...you're together. But you can't be together."

He took two small steps away from the wall.

"It's not allowed," he said and resumed pacing.

"Not allowed?" Anne asked. "What do you mean?"

"Light, dark..." The chains rattled as he punched his right fist into his left palm. "The two together. The union. One emerges."

As Hyram resumed his pacing, Dylan looked at Anne. He didn't know what they would find, but he didn't expect this. Abigail spoke to him – even demon Mary could complete a sentence – and he wasn't sure what they were going to accomplish with this. He shook his head in frustration.

Anne took a few steps forward, pulled the leather pouch from her pocket and retrieved the stone necklace. It glowed white against the darkness of the room.

"What is this?" she asked. "We know about your wife, Abigail. Do you remember your wife? Your children?"

Hyram put a hand over his mouth and stared at the necklace.

"No, no, no," he moaned. "I didn't know! How could I know?"

"Know what?" Anne asked.

"Go ahead, tell them."

Dylan and Anne turned around at the sound of Abigail's voice. She walked past the stone coffin in the center of the room and stopped within reach of her husband.

"Tell them our story, Hyram," Abigail said, her eyes full of fury. "Tell them our wonderful little fairy tale."

Hyram reached tentatively for his wife.

"The spark," Hyram said. "Your spark. Still strong." He put his head in his hands and resumed his pacing, shuffling away from Abigail as far as the chain would allow. "No, no, no, it can't be. It's not allowed."

"That's right, darling, I'm still here," Abigail said, "and full of magik! That special spark that you were so enthralled with, that you couldn't live without, that you swore you would help me nurture in our girls."

Dylan and Anne watched as Hyram Dunning let out a muffled groan and collapsed to his knees in front of his wife.

"I didn't know," he sobbed at her feet, "how could I know?"

"Tell me, darling husband," Abigail hissed, "did your life turn out like you hoped it would? Did you conquer the wilderness? Did you build your empire on the backs of others labor, just like you dreamed?"

"Abigail, I think we should –," Dylan started to say, but stopped when he saw the wild look in her eyes.

"You want to know what happened on the hill, Dylan?" Abigail hissed. "You want to know what he did, Anne?" Abigail touched Hyram gently on the chin and raised his head until he was looking directly into her eyes. "He took us, one by one, up the hill, tied us to those rocks and slit our throats."

Anne gasped and looked at Hyram with disgust, her gut instincts confirmed. She had no idea that such horror had played out on her grandfather's hill, the sacred spot where he had taught her to respect nature and all its creations. Between this, and what had happened on the hill that morning, Anne felt like a bug, trapped on its back, struggling to find its legs.

"My dreams, Abby," Hyram looked around nervously. "My dreams, I had to obey!" he pounded his head with his fists. "I didn't know!"

"Wait, I've heard that explanation before," Dylan said, suddenly angry. "Mary said that was why she killed herself. To keep from doing the terrible things she was seeing in her mind. She said she did it so she wouldn't hurt me." He walked over and grabbed Dunning by the throat. "So, you did have a choice, you piece of shit. You were just too weak to do the right thing."

Dylan squeezed harder. He acted without thinking, an instinct to protect Anne and to help Abigail and the girls. He didn't know if it was possible to kill a dead person, but he gripped Dunning's neck with both hands and relished the possibility.

"Dylan!" Anne said, but his rage was out of control. She looked at Abigail for help, but even she looked surprised.

With a strength he didn't know he possessed, Dylan pinned Hyram against the wall and then laughed as he began to struggle. Hyram's mouth opened and he let out a small squeak, unable to breathe.

"They didn't deserve to die," Dylan snarled, "you deserved to die."

Dylan felt the rage growing inside him. A rhythmic roar howled in his ear and he felt a scorching heat building inside his chest. Dylan was suddenly and horribly aware of the power surging up his spine, across his shoulders, and down into his fingertips. He pictured the raw heat leaving his body, wrapping around Dunning's throat and engulfing his body. Dylan only needed to release it – to make it real – and Hyram Dunning would be gone forever.

"Dylan," Anne said gently into his ear, "please stop."

The sound of her voice and the touch of her hand on his shoulder sent a soothing cold wave through his body. Dylan looked into Anne's eyes, and the heat of his rage quickly dissipated. He released Hyram with a shove, then walked to the other side of the room and collapsed on the floor next to Abigail.

"Abigail...I," Dylan stuttered, "...I didn't—"

"This isn't right, Dylan," Anne said, leaning against the sarcophagus with folded arms.

"What are you talking about?" Dylan asked. "What's not right?"

"None of it!" Anne said, exasperated. "What Hyram did, the fact that he's chained to the wall...you! You were completely out of control!"

Anne looked away from Dylan in disgust. Hyram had resumed his melancholic pacing, whimpering and dragging the block of concrete across the floor. It was like he didn't even know they were there.

"It's okay, Miss Leahy," a young voice said, "Dylan's a good person."

"Whoa!" Anne shouted in surprise as the two girls appeared from the shadows and stood next to their mother.

"Who—," Anne stammered, looking at the oldest girl.

"I'm Constance," she replied with a curtsy, "and this is my sister, Margaret."

"Maggie," she corrected, and also curtsied. "Do you wanna' play tag? I've wanted to play tag with someone besides my sister for so long! You're it!"

Margaret tapped Anne on the arm and bolted out the door.

"Come on," Abigail said to them both. "The three of us need to talk."

CHAPTER TWELVE

Anne sat down under the willow tree, and Dylan sat with his back against Mary's tombstone.

"How is it that the three of you are even here?" Anne asked, pointing at Abigail and the girls.

"To put it plainly," Abigail replied, "I took time, bent it like a twig, and then tied it in a knot."

"It's no use," Dylan said to Anne, "she only speaks in code about that stuff."

"Luckily, Hyram took me up the hill first," Abigail continued. "When I realized what he was doing, I made sure they didn't suffer." She sat down on the ground and leaned back against the trunk of the tree, Constance and Margaret each on a hip. She hugged them to her chest, and ran her fingers through their hair. "I tried to stop him, but the best I could do was delay the next phase, to keep us from moving on. But we can only exist here in the cemetery."

"And the chains?" Anne persisted.

"Yes, the curse was my doing," Abigail grimaced. "I wanted Hyram to have a nice welcome when he joined us here. I suppose if I had known we would all be trapped here for eternity, I might have done something different – more forgiving – but his betrayal was so complete, and so unexpected. It all happened so fast, and my first reaction was to protect the girls and..." Abigail sighed and rested her cheek on top of Margaret's head.

"Well, I don't like any of this," Anne announced emphatically. "If this is what the hill means to you, I don't want to have any part of it."

"Your grandfather's hill was a special place for people like us for millennia," Abigail said, "or so I was told by my mother and grand-mother."

"People like us?" Anne asked.

"Yes, we're all the same, Anne," Abigail said. "You, me, Dylan, my girls – we all carry the light, the energy."

"Why didn't you tell me about Hyram?" Dylan asked. "What he did?"

"You'll have to forgive me, Dylan," Abigail replied, "but this is all new to me, too. Me and the girls have always been alone. You started to show up – the first person I'd seen or spoken to in nearly 150 years – and then Mary arrived from the outer realms."

"Outer realms?" Anne asked.

"The place people with the light are supposed to go when we move on from this life," Abigail replied.

"Like Heaven," Dylan said.

"Of sorts."

"It's a place of lush green valleys, with beautiful butterflies every color of the rainbow and trees as big as mountains," Margaret said, without looking up from her mother's chest. "You can run through the forest all day long, and never reach the other side."

"It's where all bright souls go after they die," Constance added. "Not that we'll ever know."

She reached across her mother's chest and hugged her younger sister.

"So, you knew about the hill before you came here?" Anne asked.

"Hyram and I didn't come here by accident," Abigail said. "I thought I could uncover its secrets, restore its purpose on my own, but I was wrong."

"The visions," Dylan said, "Mary had them too, and Anne and I have been having dreams and – I don't know – premonitions, I guess I'd call them. Where do they come from, anyway?"

"I don't know, Dylan," Abigail said and Dylan groaned in frustration. "It wasn't something Hyram and I ever discussed, before...it never came up while we were alive. My mother used to tell me stories about the old ones, cunning folk with the gift of foresight who would see visions of possible futures. Maybe you and Anne have that gift, I don't know. But I do know about the amulet." She looked at Anne. "It was mine. It had been in my family for hundreds of years at that point, but nobody knew what the symbols meant, or how to use it to fulfill the hill's purpose."

"Again," Anne said. "What is the purpose? For me it's a place of healing, of positive energy, not a place for destruction or to be attacked by whatever that thing was."

"Thing?" Abigail asked.

"Demon Mary found us at the hill yesterday," Dylan said, "and she turned into something."

"Oh, my," Abigail said. "Reapers don't usually show their true form. They like to appear as something dark and twisted that's connected to their victim. In your case, Mary."

"Well, Mary never had a chance," Anne said. "A second reaper named Aislinn showed up and destroyed her."

Both girls snapped straight up in Abigail's lap.

"Whoa," said Margaret, "you guys saw Aislinn? What did she look like? Did she have eyes as dark as night? Did she – "

"—did she have swords?" Constance interrupted. "Did she have two black swords that shimmered like the light of a full moon?"

"Yes, she did have black eyes, actually," Dylan said and looked at Abigail, "and she definitely had two very dangerous-looking swords."

"All children with the light learn about the battles from the schism, and heroes like Aislinn," Abigail explained. "Young girls are especially fond of her."

"Forgive me," Anne chimed in, "but Aislinn is a reaper. How is it that children with the light idolize a reaper?"

"If it hadn't been for Aislinn," Abigail replied, "our kind would have been completely wiped out thousands of years ago. During the schism, she helped rally us and turned the tide at the battle of Kesh Corran."

"But demon Mary," Dylan said to Abigail, "said something about completing the circle. That we couldn't do it."

"Well, nobody has done it since before the schism," Abigail said.

"Okay, you keep talking about the schism." Anne said. "What is that all about?"

"I forget that you two are blank slates when it comes to our history,' Abigail said.

"The schism was caused by the dark energy in the universe," Constance chirped.

"Dark energy is always hungry," Margaret added.

"Yes," Abigail said and smiled. "Reapers are always hungry for bright souls, feeding on them to add to the darkness of the void, but this was more than that. The dark energy was taking control of all the planes – including this one – because we weren't maintaining our rituals in the circles of stone."

"So, the reapers are trying to take over the universe?" Dylan asked.

"I wouldn't call it that," Abigail replied. "They're just doing what they do. When an apple is ripe, it falls to the ground. The schism was a war that started when a rift opened in our plane, and the reapers came pouring through. They fed on bright souls, and darkness took root."

"Dylan, remember what I said about dark matter?" Anne said, more statement than question. "One theory about dark matter is that it's gravity from a parallel universe, disrupting our reality."

"Huh?" Dylan shook his head.

"A woman who has been dead for 150 years just described something that modern scientists only recently started talking about."

"Oh."

"Whatever it is," Abigail said, "it's why our people and our secrets have been lost to time. When we weren't being persecuted by our own kind, the reapers were hunting us down, devouring us, one by one."

"Right," Anne said, "Aislinn did tell us about that part, but that still doesn't explain what the hill is for."

"Some think the hill will open a passage to the outer realms, others think it's a weapon," Abigail said. "My mother thought it was a place of healing."

"Finally, something I agree with," Anne said. "That was the main thing I learned from my grandfather. I've always used it to find my center, for health and balance."

"Hold up, did you say the outer realms?" Dylan asked. "Isn't that where Mary is?"

"Yes," Abigail said, "but the knowledge, Dylan, it's lost."

"Mary told me that I had a special purpose and it's linked to the hill," Dylan said and grabbed Anne by the arm. "You have to help me, Anne. This could be what she meant, that I can be with her by opening a passage."

Anne felt a twinge of jealousy. The smile on his face, the excited look in his eyes. She didn't understand how he could go from probing her mouth with his tongue, to panting like a wide-eyed puppy, but it only added to the increasing foulness of this whole situation.

"Again," Abigail said, "the knowledge is lost. Nobody knows what will happen up there, or how to do it."

"When I first met you," Dylan said, "under the tree, with the journal, I saw Mary say something to you. What did she say? And don't even try to play coy, because I saw you look at her and smile."

"Her exact words were, *we think that Dylan is the key to completing the circle,"* Abigail said.

"Yes!" Dylan shouted. "So, what does that mean?"

"I don't know," Abigail said curtly, "and I'd appreciate it greatly if you'd stop asking me!"

"Fine, so teach me!" Dylan said. "Teach me how to use my powers so I can figure it out."

"Sure," Abigail's green eyes narrowed. "How about we set up a standing appointment – let's say, every other Wednesday – for the next fifty years. Does that work for you?"

Dylan groaned in frustration and pounded the earth in front of Mary's headstone.

"I'm sorry, Dylan," Anne said, "but I need some time alone. I'm just not ready for all of this." She looked at Abigail and the girls, then back at Dylan. "I think we need to go our separate ways."

"What?" Dylan objected. "You can't just leave me to deal with this alone!"

"Excuse me?" Anne responded. "I didn't ask for this, Dylan!" She stood up and brushed off the back of her pants. "I want my life back, I want my hill back and I want to sort this out – alone!"

Anne turned and walked away.

"Wait, where are you going? The first ferry to the island isn't for hours." Dylan ran up the path after Anne. "Anne, wait!"

She stopped.

"Let me walk you to the docks, okay?" Dylan asked. "Just let me see you off."

Anne motioned with her head and they walked away together.

***

The walk to the docks was a silent affair. Anne and Dylan were both exhausted – mentally and physically – and they kept their thoughts to themselves. Dylan wasn't sure what he was trying to accomplish, but at least he had delayed their separation. He just wasn't ready to say goodbye. Anne needed a hot bath and a long nap, but for some reason, she couldn't say no when he asked to tag along.

When they arrived at the docks, the first rays of sunlight were spreading their purple fingers across the horizon over Lake Huron. Cars were already beginning to cue, and people were milling about in the grass, waiting for the ticket booth to open. Dylan and Anne found an isolated bench and sat down.

As Anne watched the gentle waters of the bay, she tried to relax and let go of her anxiety. She had to admit, she *was* afraid – afraid of the reaper, of talking corpses, of change – but deep down, she knew it wasn't Dylan's fault. She couldn't explain the deep connection she felt for him, but she knew the hill was about more than him and Mary.

Dylan felt the same connection – that he and Anne had some larger purpose, a common history – but he also knew that neither of them had a fucking clue what it all meant. And that was all the reason he needed to stay focused on what Mary had told him. He needed to learn how to complete the circle, to open a portal and reunite with her in the outer realms.

Anne didn't understand how Dylan could just ignore any possible deeper meaning for the hill – for their powers – just to achieve his own purpose.

Dylan didn't understand how Anne could pretend to understand what the hill was all about, what its purpose was, when she clearly didn't know.

"How can you be so selfish," Anne said.

Dylan smirked and shook his head.

"How can you be so stubborn," he retorted.

Anne folded her arms and looked away.

"It's not just about you and Mary," Anne said.

"It's always been about me and Mary!"

"How can you say that?" Anne said incredulously. She stood up and started to pace in front of the bench. "You felt it, Dylan, we felt it together!"

"Yeah, I felt something with you up there," Dylan snickered, "and when we were naked in your cottage – I felt it then, for sure!"

Anne groaned and stood directly in front of him.

"Here," she said and took his hands, "look into my eyes and tell me what you feel."

Dylan looked up into Anne's eyes without blinking for several seconds, then his eyes got wide and he gasped in mock horror.

"I've got nothing," he said dryly.

"Exactly," Anne said and let go of his hands with a flourish. "Our connection has something to do with the hill – but it's not just about you and Mary – it's about us, too."

It wasn't that he felt nothing – he definitely felt something when he looked at Anne – it just wasn't mysterious or supernatural. No, these feelings were much more familiar. Anne was chipping away at the wall he'd built up around his heart, and he felt himself letting go, moving on.

"Anne, look," he started to say but was interrupted by a cell phone ringing.

Out of habit, Dylan reached for his pocket, then remembered that his phone didn't work. He looked at Anne with a hint of jealousy as she answered the call.

"Hello?" she said. "Yes, I'm fine, how are you today, Nancy?" Anne turned and walked up the path away from Dylan. "Yes, I do know him, actually. He's with me right now, waiting for the ferry in Eagleton. Tonight?" She looked at Dylan. "Alright, see you then."

"Nancy?" Dylan asked.

"Nancy McCoy."

"The woman who did my family tree?" Dylan asked.

"The very same," Anne replied. "She said she wants me to come over tonight because she has something for me – sorry, something for us – something very important that has to do with the hill."

"Seriously?"

Anne sat back down next to Dylan and folded her arms.

"She told me to bring you, too."

CHAPTER THIRTEEN

"Wow," Dylan said as they approached Nancy's estate, "this place is amazing."

"Yeah, I know," Anne said. "If I'd played my cards differently, this could have all been mine someday."

"How's that?"

"I was engaged to Nancy's grandson, Steven, but it didn't work out," Anne said. "Nancy is Hyram's great-granddaughter from his second marriage."

"You were engaged to one of the great-great-great-ish-grandsons of Hyram, and you didn't tell me?" Dylan said. "Don't you think that could have been helpful?"

"Do you think it's helpful, Dylan?"

"No – maybe – I don't know."

"Well, there you go," Anne said and knocked on the front door.

Aiden opened the door to the house and gestured for them to go inside.

"Nice to see you again, Miss Leahy. Mr. Ward," he said with a nod. "She's waiting for you in the study."

Aiden led Anne and Dylan into the study before announcing them. "Miss Leahy to see you, mum, with her friend –"

"Mr. Ward, yes, I'm glad I get to meet you." Nancy said and looked up from her book. She set it on the table next to her and stood up to greet them.

The study was a fairly small room, but was packed to the ceiling with rich mahogany bookshelves, filled with an eclectic mix of antique hardcover collections and modern paperbacks. Four high-backed chairs were arranged around a rectangular coffee table in front of a fireplace. The only other thing in the room that wasn't a book, was a painting that hung over the fireplace. It was a forest scene, of a small girl in a white dress, sitting under an ancient oak tree, reading a book.

"So, you already know me, eh?" Dylan asked, waving the printout of his family tree.

"Dylan!" Anne pinched his elbow and scolded him with narrow eyes. "I'm sorry, Nancy, Dylan apparently left his manners back on the mainland."

"I don't mind, dear," Nancy replied. "Please, sit down." She waited for them to each pick a chair and then settled back into her perch. "We need to talk about the hill, and your grandfather. With everything that's going on, there are things I need to tell you. Lord knows I should have told you sooner, but now especially. But first," Nancy looked at Dylan, "is there something you would like to know?"

"Anne and I were at the library doing some research on the hill, and I printed out my family history," Dylan said, more politely. "The librarian pointed you out – that you had done the research – and, I don't know, I guess I hoped you could tell me more. I'm mainly interested in the line of my family that goes back to England and ended up in Salem."

"The line of your family that carries the light?" Nancy asked.

"What?" Anne responded. "You know about that?"

"Yes, Anne," Nancy replied. "That's why I asked you here today. That hill was mine when I was a little girl – just like it was yours – long before it belonged to your grandfather. I played, I explored, just like you did. It didn't take long for me to learn that the hill was special, that there was some sort of magic up there."

"So, you have the power, too?" Dylan asked.

"No, Dylan," Nancy replied. "But Abigail – whispers of witchcraft, her power over my great-grandfather, and the like – were quietly discussed in these halls. My obsession with the hill, with ancient religions, occultism – that's Abigail's influence on me. Even though we weren't related, and her name was scorned, I never shared that view. I wanted to know more."

"When did you and Anne's grandfather become friends?"

"We were more than friends," Nancy said with a wink.

"Oh," Dylan said, "so, you two were...you know..."

"Dylan!" Anne scolded.

"Lovers, yes," Nancy said.

"Wait, really?" Anne said. "I mean, I guess I always suspected, but neither of you ever told me directly. When was this?"

"It started one summer during the war," Nancy continued. "My husband and I decided it would be wise to liquidate some of our assets with the war on, and your grandfather had just purchased the island from us. While my husband was away fighting the Germans, your grandfather and I spent the summer together, enjoying life, the island," Nancy looked at Dylan, "each other."

"Wait," Dylan said, "Germans? World War II? How old are you?"

"Dylan!"

"I'm ninety-seven," Nancy replied with a distant look, "but I'm not too old to remember the way he made me feel, or how he took my breath away on those long summer days together on the hill."

"Okay, I never would have guessed you were ninety-seven," Dylan said and looked at Anne, "if that helps."

"I think that's the healing power of the hill," Nancy replied. "It's not a fountain of youth, but I think Anne would agree there is a calming, peaceful energy that is very soothing up there. I have no doubt its added years to my life."

"So, what happened with your husband?" Dylan asked.

"That's the funny thing about war – when your entire world is turned upside down, and there's a chance it will be completely destroyed, or simply changed forever – you do things you would never do otherwise." Nancy said solemnly. "The time I spent with Gavin, your grandfather," she said to Anne, "was a way for me to cope with a situation I had absolutely no hope of controlling. When my husband came back from the war that autumn, it just ended, and life went on back in New York."

"Alright, so what does this have to do with my family tree, exactly?" Dylan asked.

"It all has to do with your family tree, Dylan," Nancy said. She stood up and flipped a switch on the mantle over the fireplace, and the portrait of the little girl began to rise into the ceiling. Behind the portrait was a large flat screen display. Nancy touched a few icons on the screen and Dylan's family tree appeared.

She retrieved a small tablet from a drawer of the end-table and sat back down. With a few swipes of her fingers, two more family trees appeared, superimposed over Dylan's. Wherever the three different webs coalesced into a single point, they were highlighted in red.

"You, Abigail, and Anne share a line that has long been associated with witchcraft, at least as far back as I've been able to document. You all come from the same female ancestor in Ireland. This whole tangled web boils down to her and her children, a boy and a girl, but I don't know anything about her. That's where the trail ended."

Nancy tapped the tablet and the family trees were replaced with a map of the world.

"Wow," Dylan said, standing up and peering at the screen. "What do the different shades of blue mean?"

"It's a heat map," replied Nancy. "The darker the color, the greater the concentration of ancestors. Here, this should help paint the picture for you."

Arrows appeared on the screen that created a network of trails from Central Europe, over to the Atlantic coast of Spain and France, across the English Channel into Great Britain, and finally across the ocean to North America.

"There are three branches of your family trees that have the most common ancestors," Nancy continued. "They arrived in the Western Hemisphere in two main areas: from the British Isles into Salem, and from Spain to South America via Mexico."

As Anne watched and listened to Nancy, she felt duped. She didn't doubt Nancy's intentions, but it was hard to understand why such a huge – literally life changing – secret had been kept from her all these years. It wasn't like she was a little girl anymore. Why hadn't her grandfather told her? And the technology? Using words like '*heat map*?' Really? As refined and capable as Nancy had always appeared, the touch screen and tablet seemed like props in a bad detective show.

"Nancy, how did you...?" Anne pointed at the screen.

"What?" Nancy replied. "You think I'm too old to learn a few computer programs? I didn't survive all these years by letting other people do *everything* for me."

"So, this is nice, and all," Dylan said, "but if we wanted to try to find someone else – one of our relatives – to talk to about all of this, how would we even start?"

"Oh," Nancy said. "Here are all the living relatives, mapped by their last known address. Hold on, it might take a minute because there's a lot of data in play here."

Dots began to appear all over the map, with concentrations of dark blue color in Central Mexico, and around Boston. Dylan put his hands on the mantle and peered at the screen as the dots combined into clusters in Ireland, England and Wales, all across Central and Eastern Europe, into Asia, India, Australia, and Africa.

"How is this helping?" Dylan asked. "There are people, literally, all over the world. How many are there, anyway?"

"About fifty-thousand," Nancy said.

"On a planet with eight billion people?" Anne said quietly. "No wonder the old ways have been forgotten. To your point, though, Dylan," she stood up and joined him by the screen, "we would probably look around Boston, since the Salem line was one of our most consistent. Can we zoom in, Nancy?"

"Just touch the screen, dear," she replied. "Like Google maps."

Anne fought through the strangeness of hearing those words come from Nancy's mouth, touched the screen, panned over to Boston and zoomed into the area around Salem. The clusters again became single dots, and names appeared next to them.

"This is actually a pretty reasonable number of people to start with," Anne said. "What do you think, there's maybe a couple dozen?"

"So, what?" Dylan said. "We just start knocking on doors and say *'hi, I'm your long lost relative, do you see dead people?'* I've got relatives in Boston, and trust me, that wouldn't go over well."

"Really," Anne said, "where, in Boston?"

"Over here," Dylan said, panning the screen, "he's on the north side, kind of by the, oh, fucking hell."

"Martin Ward?" Anne asked.

"Uncle Marty," Dylan said, repeatedly tapping his forehead on the mantle. "Are you telling me that he has the same superpowers as we do?"

"It's impossible to say," Nancy replied. "Who has the gift, how it's passed down through the generations is still a mystery. Why is it apparent in Anne, but not her parents or grandparents?"

"Well," Dylan replied, "I'll tell you what I know. My Uncle Marty is certifiable. He's a hoarder and a life-long bachelor who's lived in my grandma's house since the day he got back from Vietnam."

"When was the last time you saw him?" Anne asked.

"I was eleven," Dylan said. "It was the first Christmas dinner after grandma died. Let's just say that he and my dad had too much to drink, and they settled it out on the front lawn with their fists." He looked up at the screen and shook his head. "We never went back."

"Hmm," Anne said and panned around on the screen. "There are others, I guess. There are a couple of people right up in Salem, actually."

Nancy went over to the bookshelf, retrieved a book, then placed it on the table next to Anne. "Although our romance ended, your grandfather and I had a special friendship, every summer, for the rest of his life."

"Whoa," Anne said. She sat back down and gently ran her hand across the worn, leather book. A spiral pattern, with straight lines coming out of the center, was on the cover. "That's the symbol from the cave!" Anne opened the book and carefully began turning the pages. "Wait," she said pointing at the text, "that's my grandfather's handwriting. Was this his book?"

"In a manner of speaking, yes," Nancy replied, "All my life, I've been on the lookout for books on the occult, spiritualism, and ancient religions," Nancy said. "I found this in a little bookstore in the Irish countryside, not far from where I had traced your ancestors. The book was a bit of an enigma when I bought it. It had been cross-referenced against every known megalith and standing stone site in Europe, but nothing was ever directly tied to the details it contained. I recognized immediately that it had information about the hill – our hill – and I gave it to your grandfather to study. He insisted that I keep it here, but he used to spend hours studying the runes, trying to make sense of the symbols and the pictures."

"It looks like a grimoire," Anne said, flipping through the pages, "a book of spells and ceremonies that all have to do with the hill," she explained to Dylan. "Look here, at the top of each page" she pointed at a picture of the moon and stars. "This must be telling you when to conduct the ceremony and then the instructions and spell work are below, with different combinations of symbols from the stones." Anne shook her head. "It would take years to figure this out."

"Your grandfather spent a lifetime," Nancy said, "but he was able to figure out a few things from trial and error. Which plants the pictures refer to, for example. Some of your favorite recipes and spells came from this book."

"Yeah, I can see that," Anne said, "on this page next to a picture of the hill and the stone circle, he refers to a recipe that he used to brew a special tea for Samhain." Anne sighed. "I guess Dr. Parsons was right.

Without a way to translate the symbols, we'll never know what was supposed to happen up there."

"Taganna dorchadas, eadrama solaras," Dylan pointed at the page.

"What did you just say?" Anne asked.

"The symbols on the stones," Dylan said. "Don't you see the picture?"

"What are you talking about?" Anne asked.

"The symbols on the stones are flat, two-dimensional, but if you think of them in three dimensions, they join together. Like a puzzle."

"I'm not seeing this, Dylan," Anne turned the book sideways.

"Even when I look at the symbols on the totem, that's what I see," Dylan explained, pulling the piece of wood from his pocket. "I see a picture in three dimensions, and I hear those words: taganna dorchadas, eadrama solaras."

"You're just telling me this now?"

"Do you know what it means?"

"No."

"Well, there you go."

"I think I recognize some of those words," Nancy interjected. "Solara is clearly the sun, maybe dorchadas is the moon?"

"No," Anne said tapping her phone, "according to Google, dorchadas is Gaelic for darkness. I'll try to translate it. What was the phrase again?"

"Taganna dorchadas, eadroma solaras," Dylan repeated.

"Hmm," Anne said, "it's not an exact match, but it looks like it says, 'as darkness falls, light emerges,' or something like that."

"Brilliant," Dylan went back to the display, "we've unraveled all of the mysteries of the universe."

"Nancy..." Anne ran her fingers across the book, but struggled to find the words.

"Gavin insisted we keep the truth from you," Nancy said, apparently reading Anne's mind. "He said that you would find out when the time was right."

"Hey, wait," Dylan tapped at the screen with his fingers. "Why is there a red dot next to my Uncle Marty's name?"

"Just a moment, and I'll tell you." Nancy flipped a switch next to the mantle and it descended back into place. "Do you like my painting, Anne?"

"It's lovely," Anne replied. "Seems appropriate for a library."

"On purely artistic merit, I think we can agree it's mediocre at best," Nancy continued, "but it used to sit on the wall in the childhood home of Charles Lutwidge Dodgson, who grew up to write as Lewis Carroll."

"Alice in Wonderland?" Anne noticed a dark hole near the roots of the tree, partially obscured by tufts of grass and a small green shrub. "This must be worth a fortune."

"It is, my dear," Nancy said, "especially considering that only a handful of people know it exists." She settled back into her chair. "As I said, I've had a lifelong obsession with anything associated with the hill. When I watched Erik Larson's video, and saw his ridiculous behavior afterward, I did a little digging."

"And?" Anne prompted.

"There was a stone," Nancy continued, "a crystal that was used on the hill. Your friend Erik Larson found it in the cave, on the altar in front of the carving. He was trying to sell it."

"Bastard," Anne sneered.

"The bright white rock, Anne." Dylan tapped the page of the book, where the two figures knelt together in front of an altar, streams of light radiating in every direction. "There, on the capstone. We both saw it in our visions. So, did you get it?" Dylan looked at Nancy. "Did you buy it from him?"

"Unfortunately, no," Nancy waved her hand. "The bidding war was just starting when I was told the crystal had been sold."

"That's it, Anne," Dylan pointed at the book again, "it has to be. If we have the stone, we should be able to complete what was started up there and open up a portal."

"We don't know that it's a portal," Anne said. "It could be a place of healing, or it could be a weapon. What if it releases a horde of reapers? What if it alters reality, or destroys us all together?"

"No, Anne," Dylan shook his head, "nothing we've seen, nothing we've felt has been like that. It's about opening a portal, whatever that means."

"Exactly, Dylan," Anne said, "thank you for proving my point. We don't know what it means!"

"So, who has it?" Dylan asked Nancy.

"Ordinarily, it doesn't work like that, I'm afraid." Nancy smiled. "Discreet transactions like this don't include the names of other interested parties, and certainly not the new owner. But there was someone I suspected, a polite rival of mine."

"Polite rival?" Anne slumped down in a chair.

"Suspected, as in past-tense?" Dylan sat down with his arms on his knees. "You don't think they have it?"

"She, Dylan." Nancy passed a small, hand-written note to him. "I know she has it, because she sent me this."

Dylan read the note and gave it to Anne.

Send them to me

Soon

A

"A?" Anne put the note on the coffee table.

"To those within her circle, she's known as Airmid."

"Airmid?" Dylan asked.

"The Irish goddess of healing and herbalism," Nancy replied.

"Wait, by circle," Anne picked the note back up, "you mean, coven?"

"Yes," Nancy said, "she recruited me long before I met your grandfather. She knew about the hill, and my interest in unraveling its secrets. I've always resisted her advances, politely declined her requests, save one. I'm the acting guardian of this site, your grandfather's hill."

"This site?" Dylan asked. "You mean there's more than one?"

"The dark blue areas on the map, remember? People that carry the light seem to be drawn to them, even when they don't know they exist, or that they have the power at all." Nancy tapped at the screen of her tablet and a printer whirred to life. "There's a network of sites, all over the world. Most have been deliberately hidden, like the one on your hill, were intentionally destroyed, or have simply been lost to the elements."

"And the red dot?"

"I can't speak to your Uncle's powers or lack thereof," Nancy gave the printout to Dylan, "but the red dot means that he is part of Airmid's coven. That has the names and addresses of everyone in my database within 30 miles of Boston."

"There's only like five red dots next to all these names," Dylan pointed at the paper.

"Rather than inspire loyalty, Airmid has always demanded it, and that's not a good way to make friends," Nancy explained. "It probably would be a good idea to talk to your uncle first," she continued, "that way he could introduce you to Airmid. It might be easier to meet her with a familiar face in the room."

"So, what?" Anne looked over Dylan's shoulder at the printout. "We just run off to see her in Salem?"

"She sent the message through me as a courtesy, requesting your presence," Nancy said. "If you don't comply, she'll bring you in."

"What," Dylan shook his head, "like a mobster?"

"No, like a witch."

CHAPTER FOURTEEN

Anne and Dylan sat on the front porch steps of Anne's cottage and looked out at the horizon. The waves from Lake Huron rolled gently onto the rocks of the inlet. It was a clear night, and far from any city lights, the stars blanketed the night sky.

Anne set her grandfather's book on the porch beside her, the printout of names and addresses folded inside like a bookmark. For Anne, the conversation with Nancy had changed everything and nothing all at the same time. She was still reeling, trying to understand why Nancy and her grandfather had kept all those secrets. Especially her grandfather. Why would he teach her about the hill, expose its healing touch, but not mention its deeper meaning?

She still wanted to be alone, to go back to her solitary life with the hill and the predictable subtlety of earth's natural cycles, but as she looked at the man sitting next to her on the porch, she knew that was all changing, too.

And change wasn't always bad.

"Look," Anne broke the silence and pointed at the sky. "Cassiopeia."

"Cassie, what now?"

"Cassiopeia, the big W," she repeated, then took Dylan's hand and traced the pattern of the constellation. "Don't you know that story?"

Dylan shook his head.

"Cassiopeia was the queen of Ethiopia, and by all accounts was very beautiful. Helen of Troy was a looker, but deep down she just wanted to be loved. Cassiopeia, on the other hand, had a nasty little vain streak. It wasn't enough that she was gorgeous, she needed everyone to say it out loud, and to treat her that way, too. Eventually, she claimed that she was more beautiful than all the nymphs of the sea, and that invoked the wrath of Poseidon."

"Yikes," Dylan said, "the one with the trident?"

"Yeah," replied Anne, "you don't wanna fuck with Poseidon's posse of sea nymphs. As punishment, Poseidon had Cassiopeia tied to a chair, her arms above her shoulders, her chest laid bare. And that's her," Anne pointed to the stars with her free hand and traced the pattern again, "arms bound, stretched across the heavens for all eternity."

"Bare chest?" Dylan asked. "Is she the one that squirts milk across the sky?"

"No," Anne replied, "that's a different set of boobs all together, but if it makes you remember the story, then by all means."

"I had no idea so much drama had been shining down on me all these years," Dylan said.

"Alright, your turn," Anne said.

"Aha," Dylan pointed, "the Big Dipper!"

"Hmm," Anne teased. "AKA the plow. You go from topless queens to plowing fields. Horny much?"

"Hey, you asked," Dylan said defensively. "I just kinda suck at star stuff, that's all. Go on then," he nudged her gently, "do another one."

"Alright," she said, "Cygnus the Swan." She traced the pattern with her fingertips. "Also known as the Northern Cross."

"That's it?" Dylan asked. "No treachery or intrigue?"

"Nope, just a swan, showing the way." She used her hand to make a small explosion on the side of her head and giggled.

"So, how did you learn so much about the stars?"

"Up here," Anne said, "another thing I learned from my grandfather. He was always in tune with the seasons, the cycles of the moon, and the stars and planets. It's a big part of my beliefs, my craft."

She stopped and looked at Dylan, searching his face for a trace of the intolerance she imagined was festering just under the surface, but he just looked back at her, smiled and looked back up at the night sky.

"It sounds like you learned a lot from him," Dylan said.

"I did," Anne replied, "and looking back, going to New York with Steven after college was a huge mistake. I wish I'd stayed here, to learn as much as I could, and to be there with him at the end."

"How did he die?"

"A stroke," Anne wiped a tear from the corner of her eye. "It was weeks before anyone missed him and came to check on him. They found him up on the hill, leaning against the oak tree with a bag full of moldy raspberries."

"That must have been really hard to deal with," Dylan said. "Wait, did you say raspberries? That's what I brought to you that first night. I'm so sorry."

"It's fine," she said, "you didn't know. Yes, the raspberries immediately reminded me of my grandfather, but it's okay, it made me feel good, and in a weird way, actually helped me trust you. What happened to Mary really tore you up, didn't it?"

"Before I met you, I," he paused and scratched his chin, "I thought I could drink my pain away. That by being numb, I wouldn't have to deal with what Mary did, let alone move on."

"You don't look like someone who's chained to a bottle."

"I'm not anymore," Dylan said. "After Abigail rescued me in the cemetery, I spent a couple months in some sort of hole surrounded by bright light. I think she was healing me, but whatever she did, when I came back out, I didn't want to drink anymore."

"A couple of months?"

"Yeah," Dylan replied. "It felt like I spent a couple of hours there and then took a nap, but when I woke up, the summer was over. That's when I came to the island to see the hill."

"Well," Anne said, "the light can heal, I can attest to that, but clearly it also has something to do with controlling the flow of time. If black holes can warp space-time with their gravity, maybe the light is a way of keeping out the dark matter. Like how trees grow."

"Trees?"

"When they grow in a forest, they tend to go straight up to find the sunlight," Anne said, "but when they have more space, they throw their limbs out along the ground, stabilizing their trunks, and growing in all directions."

"I don't follow."

"It's like Abigail said," Anne said. "Since our light isn't doing what it's supposed to do, the dark matter is spreading out, growing into our plane and taking over."

"So, what about you," Dylan changed the subject. "I assume your grandfather left all of this to you?"

"He did, but I stayed away for years after he died," Anne said. "I threw myself into my work, traveled constantly, collected a fat paycheck and surrounded myself with nice things. But it wasn't enough, because I felt completely disconnected from the universe. I mean, look," she swept her hand across the horizon. "How can you not feel connected to all of this?"

"I don't know," Dylan said. "Every day the sun comes up, and every night the stars come out. I guess I've just always taken it for granted. So, that's how you know about black holes and that...other stuff?"

"Dark matter," replied Anne. "Yeah, I can't say I understand all the math behind it, but it's always been a hobby of mine."

"So, where's the nearest black hole?" Dylan asked, suddenly quiet.

"The center of our galaxy, I guess. Are you scared, Dylan?"

"Shitless."

"Me, too."

Anne took Dylan's hand and scooted over until her head was touching his shoulder. The familiar spark of their bond began to warm her skin.

"That feels good," he said.

"Is this alright?" Anne asked. "Do you mind?"

"Yeah, it's fine."

They sat together and stared at the sky without talking.

"I didn't ask for any of this, you know," Dylan said after a few minutes. "Not Mary, Abigail and her girls, meeting you. None of it."

"Me, either," Anne said. "Before I met you, I just wanted to enjoy my summer and be left alone. There's a part of me that still wants to be left alone, but the truth is, I wasn't really happy by myself."

Anne listened to the sound of the waves lapping at the rocks, and she realized that was a huge understatement. Celeste was right, Nancy was right – hell, even Sheriff Jenkins was right – she needed to reengage, to let people in again. She squeezed Dylan's hand.

"Now that I'm part of whatever is going on here," Dylan said, "I want to know more. I want to fix whatever went wrong up on the hill. I want to be able to – "

"—see Mary again," interrupted Anne, "yes, I know."

Anne wasn't trying to be mean, but she immediately regretted the words.

"Anne, if your grandfather had come back – if he talked to you about the hill, its purpose – wouldn't you want to see him, wouldn't you want to try to do what he said you should do?"

"Of course, I would," she said. "Who wouldn't want a chance to see someone they love one more time? But you and I both know it's about more than that with Mary. Your feelings for her are clouding your judgement. This isn't just about you being able to see Mary. It's more than that."

"Okay, I admit that at first, I just wanted to see her," Dylan said, "like I had been granted some crazy wish, and I would be able to go on living with my dead wife. But after I saw her – really saw her – and she told me about the hill, everything changed. She told me that to figure this all out, I'd have to let her go. It's still about her, but it's different."

"Alright," replied Anne, "I get that, I guess."

"I'll always have feelings for Mary, but that doesn't mean..."

Dylan trailed off and stared at the sky.

"Doesn't mean, what?" Anne prompted.

"It doesn't mean that I can't have feelings again," he said, "that I don't have feelings for you."

"There were a lot of negatives in that sentence, Dylan," Anne lifted her head so she could look into his eyes. "Are you saying you have feelings for me?"

"Yes," he said. "I know there's something bigger going on here, but besides that, there's something about you. You're the first person I've met since Mary died that makes me feel."

"Feel what?"

"Feel," Dylan repeated. "I used to think that Mary was my soul mate – I still do, I guess – but that was before you touched me and my whole body came alive, before I looked into your eyes and felt the passion of a thousand lifetimes, before you kissed me and – "

"Okay, okay," Anne put a hand on his mouth. She put her head on his shoulder and snuggled closer. "Me, too. You're the first person I've met since moving here that I didn't want to chase off with a baseball bat."

"Or a shotgun?"

"Exactly."

Anne giggled.

"It's not that simple, though, is it?" Dylan rubbed Anne's shoulder. "These feelings, our connection, it's not natural. We only just met, for fuck's sake."

"It's definitely not normal," she replied. "I mean, the spark is just..."

She traced a gentle arc across Dylan's kneecap with her fingertips.

"Easy!" Dylan grabbed her hand. "I feel like I'm twelve years old at the school dance. I'm not sure I have control of all my, uh, bits and pieces."

Anne laughed and Dylan moved his hand down her arm, playfully tickling at her hip. The warmth of his touch surged into her abdomen and rippled between her legs.

"Whoa," Anne broke free of Dylan's grasp and stood up. "Okay, I see what you mean. Maybe we need to have a no touching around the waist rule."

"Yeah," Dylan agreed, "that's probably best."

"Whew," Anne fanned at her face with her hands and looked at the water. "Up for a swim?"

"Lake Huron, in October?" Dylan stood up. "No, thanks."

"Oh, come on." She stepped out of her shoes, shimmied out of her jeans and threw her shirt on Dylan's lap. "The water's had all summer to warm up," she said as she padded over to the footbridge, "and besides, the inlet is always warmer than the open lake."

She jumped into the water and let out a yelp that echoed through the trees.

Dylan walked over to the footbridge and tested the water with his hand.

"It's not too bad, I guess."

"I told you," Anne looked up from the water and splashed Dylan's leg. "Don't be shy. I've already seen you, remember? It's okay if you go turtle, I know you've got nothing to be ashamed of." Anne submerged and swam away, out toward the rocks at the mouth of the inlet.

Dylan stripped down to his boxer briefs, then leapt in after her.

"Holy, fuck!" he said after he bobbed back up to the surface. "This is so much colder than you made it seem."

Anne found a large boulder near the mouth of the inlet and sat down. She loved to sit here in the summer, half submerged, and look up at the stars, or soak up the sun, while still comfortably under the water.

"Nice spot," Dylan said and sat down next to her.

"It's like having my own private window to the universe." Anne pointed up at the moon. "The moon is waxing. That means it's a good time to start new things."

"New things, like drinking tea instead of coffee, or a new flavor of soda?"

"Sure, or sitting half naked in Lake Huron in October with your new lady friend, trying not to shiver." Anne hugged her knees to her chest. "I don't want to say goodbye, Dylan. I want to figure out what all of this means, too, but it can't just be about you. This connection, our light, it's about us. Do you understand?"

"I do," he said. "But you also have to know that Mary is part of who I am, and she's still part of why I'm doing all of this."

"Alright, then," replied Anne. "I guess we're going to Boston."

"I wish it was that easy," Dylan threw a small stone into the water. "I don't have the money for a trip like that. Hell, I don't even have a place to live right now. I guess I could jump back into working at the restaurant."

"Restaurant?"

"Yeah, my friend Kyle owns the *Traveler's Hearth* over in Eagleton and gave me a job after Mary died. The tourist season is over now, but I'm sure he'd put me back to work." Dylan explained how Kyle and Edy had helped him out after he met Abigail and was evicted from his apartment.

"Well," Anne said. "Don't give that a second thought. You can crash with me until we figure this all out. And don't worry, I'll pay for your ticket."

"Anne, no," Dylan objected.

"Shush," she replied and ran her fingertips through her damp hair. "It's just money, and besides, we need to focus on what's important."

"Unlocking the secrets of the universe?"

"Exactly," Anne smiled and started to swim away. "Last one to the cottage has to make dinner!"

CHAPTER FIFTEEN

Anne knocked on Marty's front door and she and Dylan waited on the porch. The door creaked open and a wrinkled face peeked out from the edge of the storm door. He looked Anne and Dylan up and down, peering with his one good eye.

He grunted.

"You, I know," he pointed at Anne. "I recognize you from the internet."

He pushed his head further out the door and poked Dylan in the chest with a beat-up black cane. "Who are you, and why are you bothering me?" Dylan felt a familiar twinge of uneasiness as Marty covered his good eye and stared with the foggy, gray orb that used to be his left eye. It seemed to hold secrets – dark, horrible secrets about war, death and broken promises – that even today, as an adult, made Dylan uncomfortable. No, not uncomfortable. Unworthy.

"Very funny, Uncle Marty," Dylan said. "Sorry we're late, but traffic in this town is unreal."

"Ah, Mikey's little brat." Marty continued the ruse. He moved his head up and down, pretending to look harder. "Didn't recognize you after all these years." Marty turned around and mumbled under his breath as he ambled away from the door – most likely riddled with profanities, and without a doubt, concerning the nature of Dylan's genitals.

Anne and Dylan followed him into the house. The faint smell that had floated through the front door became a torrent of musty decay and neglected cleanliness. Cardboard boxes and plastic totes filled every inch of the walls, with just enough space to walk on the floor. It was clear that many small, furry creatures had lived, died and decayed in this rodent's paradise. To their right, boxes were stacked to the ceiling in the living room, with piles of newspapers, magazines and books balancing on top.

On their left, the dining room was similarly packed, with mountains of what looked like Dylan's grandmother's clothes heaped on the table and draped over the chairs.

"Wow," Dylan said. "I love what you've done with the place."

Marty abruptly turned, took two steps toward Dylan, and his left eye began to twitch.

"Easy," Dylan raised his hands. "It's just, I haven't been here since that Christmas."

"The night I kicked your dad's pansy ass right out of my life," Marty replied. "You think I can't take *you*? A wispy little twat whose first thought is to throw up his hands?"

"I'm not a kid, anymore," Dylan said and grabbed Marty's shirt with both hands.

"Gentlemen," Anne said, wedging between them. "As much as I love family reunions, I think we need to stay focused on what's important. The reason we're here, remember?"

Dylan let go of Marty's shirt with a shove. Without responding, Marty walked down the hall into the kitchen, supporting his left leg with his cane. Dirty dishes were stacked in the sink and on top of the counters, with used frozen dinner containers, open tin cans, and empty whiskey bottles poised to crash to the floor at any moment. Marty sat down at the small, folding table in the center of the room and took a cigarette from the pack sitting next to an overstuffed ashtray. He pointed at an empty chair across from him.

"One of you will need to stand," he said. He lit the cigarette, took a long drag, and looked at Dylan. "I assume that honor will fall to your bodyguard?"

Marty found a cup of coffee hidden in a heap of used paper plates and took a sip.

"You're late, but there's still time if you want a quick sip of motor oil," he said to Anne.

She glanced around the kitchen briefly before replying. She caught a glimpse of gray hair, and an overflowing trash bag in the corner began to rustle.

"No, thank you," she said politely and then sat down across from him. "We grabbed something on the way over from the airport."

"So, do you have the power, Uncle Marty?" Dylan leaned against the wall next to a yellow, corded telephone.

"Power?"

"You know, *the light.*" Dylan air quoted the words, like it would help explain their deeper meaning.

Marty took another long drag from his cigarette and eyed his nephew.

"What do you know about the light?" Marty asked.

"Not much," Dylan replied, "but we know that we both have some sort of power. A bond, that draws us together."

"Didn't your dad have that talk with you?" Marty shook his head. "That ain't some cosmic power, boy, it's human nature." He looked at Anne across the table. "Just stick it in her and get it over with, so you can both get on with your lives."

"This isn't a joke." Anne's eyes narrowed. "This is a real thing, Marty. We've seen things." She paused and looked at Dylan over her shoulder and he nodded his head. "Some sort of creature attacked us on my grandfather's hill, something that can't just be explained away or dismissed with the wave of a hand. We need help figuring it out, and we hope that Airmid can help us."

Marty scoffed.

"Power," he scoffed and flicked the end of his cigarette over the ashtray. "More like curse, but yeah, she knows about the power, and yeah, she'll have answers for you." He looked from Anne to Dylan. "But you won't like 'em."

"Well, this Airmid asked to see us," Dylan said, "so she must know something."

"You'd do well to learn your place, for starters." Marty inhaled deeply and blew a cloud of smoke at the ceiling. "This Airmid, you ignorant twit, is a woman that demands respect, and for good reason. You'll want to address her as Mistress Airmid, and when you answer a question, it's 'yes, Mistress' or 'no, Mistress,' got it?"

"Okay, good to know."

"How long have you known her?" Anne asked.

"Oh, I don't know, exactly." He tapped his finger against the side of the coffee cup and looked at the ceiling. "Twenty-five, going on thirty years now, I guess. I met her in the early 80's at a yoga class my VA counselor recommended. She was the instructor."

"If you and I both have the gift, why didn't my mom and dad ever say anything about it? Did they have it too?"

"No, your folks don't have the light," Marty replied, "but man, I'd love to see the look on your dad's face if you asked him about it. When we were kids, he used to make fun of me because I'd wake up screaming from nightmares, and my body would tingle when we'd go hiking every summer up in the mountains. The same spot, on a hill overlooking the lake, like fucking clockwork."

"We've had dreams, and visions together, too," Anne said. "They feel so real. You've had them your whole life?"

"Yeah, they followed me everywhere, even to the jungles of Vietnam." Marty said. "One night we were pinned down at the base of some God forsaken hill near the border of Laos, and I had a dream about..." Marty paused, looked at Anne and then pointed at his bad eye. "Me, Ramblin Joe, and Schmidty were the only ones in my platoon to make it off that fucking hill."

"Yes," Anne said politely, "Dylan told me about your service – but the dreams, your vision – it must have happened other times as well. How have you coped with that all your life?"

"I don't have to cope anymore, thanks to Rebecca." He took one last pull from his cigarette and then tapped it out. "She pulled the light right out of me, and I'm better off for it. No visions, no nightmares, no tingles. All that's left are the demons I made myself. Speaking of which, come on." He pulled himself up and steadied his weight on his cane. "Thanks to you, we have to battle the afternoon rush, and we can't keep her waiting."

***

After parking the car, they walked a few blocks and found themselves smack in the middle of Salem's occult district. Stores peddling pagan supplies, books, traditional tourist knick-knacks, designer coffee and up-scale sandwiches lined both sides of the street. There was a dark, new-age vibe to the entire scene, and it was impossible to forget why this town was famous the world over. References to witchcraft – signs advertising fortune tellers, palm reading, and tarot – were everywhere.

Marty led them to a small, unassuming storefront, painted in flat, black paint. A single large window was covered with a dark purple curtain, with a small hand-written sign that said, 'fortunes told,' propped in front. The solid wooden door, also painted completely black, had a small bell rigged above it on the doorframe, which announced their arrival as they stepped inside. A few tables and display cases were organized around the perimeter of the dimly lit parlor, filled with chalices, small ornamental knives, books on the history and current practice of witchcraft, and small baskets of gemstones and essential oils. Another purple curtain, identical to the one in the window was draped across a doorway at the back of the room. A quiet conversation lilted through from the other side of the curtain, but the words were too faint to understand.

"She's with a client," a young girl with light blue hair and a piercing above her eye said from behind the counter. "You can have a seat, if you like."

Marty sat down, while Anne began gently fingering the gemstones and taking the caps off the small bottles of oil to sample their fragrance.

Dylan stood and waited, trying to place the familiar scent of the incense burning on the glass counter next to the antique cash register.

"I swear I've smelled that before. What is it?" he asked the girl.

"It's a special blend," she replied. "It helps to cleanse and open the mind before readings."

"Oh, we're not here for a reading."

"I know." She smiled again and looked at Marty. "Hey, Marty."

After a few minutes, a young man and a woman emerged from behind the curtain. The man's face was flushed, and the woman's eyes were puffy and bloodshot. They walked quietly out of the store, save for the ringing of the bell, and the young girl with blue hair shut and locked the door behind them.

"This way," the girl said, holding back the curtain.

The room behind the curtain was even darker than the front of the store, lit only by candles that formed a ring around the perimeter of the room. There were several high-backed chairs, with rich mahogany trim and purple velvet cushions, surrounding a small round table with a crystal ball, a deck of Tarot cards, and a large black pillar candle that had just been extinguished.

A young woman sat in one of the chairs, her back ramrod straight, and long blonde hair flowing gently over her left shoulder. She wore a dazzling red gown, trimmed with satin and lace, and sat with one leg crossed seductively over the other. Her bare feet and painted black toenails begged for attention, but Dylan couldn't tear his gaze away from the woman's plunging neckline, where a black and red serpent wound itself around a wooden stake between her perfectly proportioned breasts, pushed up over the edges of her dress, like two ripe apples.

"Hi, we're here to see Mistress Airmid?" Dylan sat down on the nearest chair, confused.

The woman snorted in the back of her throat and then chuckled at the ceiling.

"Did Martin tell you to call me that?" She narrowed her eyes and smiled in his direction. "You're such a little card, Martin Ward. It never ceases to amaze me how someone so broken and pathetic can be so full of humor. Priceless." She looked back at Dylan. "No, darling, it's been centuries since anyone called me by my craft name. You can call me Rebecca – Mistress Rebecca, if you must – but never, ever, call me Becky."

Dylan felt a familiar squeeze, like a warning shot fired across his groin, and he wondered if all teenage girls with the light were taught this defensive skill by their mothers when they came of age. But then, the pressure began to move, probing and exploring the length and breadth of Dylan's manhood, and he found himself suddenly and uncontrollably aroused.

"I'm sorry, did you say centuries?" Dylan put his hands in his lap and shifted uncomfortably in his chair. "Exactly how old are – " He stopped when Anne kicked him in the shin. "Again, many apologies, Mistress – I mean, Rebecca – but, you don't look a day over twenty-five, and our friend Nancy said she has known you since Stalin, and Uncle Marty here met you like, thirty years ago."

"What Dylan is trying to ask, Rebecca," Anne jumped in so Dylan didn't completely swallow his foot, "is how someone with your ample life experience, can appear so healthy and balanced. You're simply radiant."

"Fearless, yet diplomatic." Rebecca raised an eyebrow. "Your grandfather was neither, alas. We could have been such good friends, he and I, if he hadn't been such a stubborn, ignorant rube."

Despite the insult, Anne returned Rebecca's gaze without moving a single muscle in her face. Anne's polite smile remained glued to her cheeks, and her eyes seemed to blink in slow motion. She waited patiently, primed by the confidence of years of successful high-stakes negotiations. Marty picked absently at the flesh around his fingernails, and Dylan seemed to be the only one moving in the room, looking back and forth between Rebecca and Anne. Dylan knew better than to say something, but he could tell that Rebecca's comment had found its mark, because Anne's cheeks were visibly flushed.

After a few more awkward moments of silence, Rebecca inhaled through her nose and exhaled slowly out of her mouth.

"Yes, yes," she said at last, waving her hand dismissively, "it's true. I'm really fucking old. My mother was Petronella de Meath, burned at the stake in 1324 in Kilkenny for witchcraft. I learned most of what I know about the light from her, and everything else because of her conniving cunt of an employer, the late Lady Alice Kyteler.."

"Kilkenny, so you're from Ireland?" Dylan perked up.

"Jaysus, Marty, I don't baleevit." A sarcastic brogue oozed out the side of Rebecca's mouth. "I taught ya were stretchin it, but he really is a daft pellet, i'nne?" She looked back at Dylan. "Is there any other Kilkenny, ya pea wit?"

"It's just that," Dylan continued, "we have a lot of questions about our superpowers, and we both have ancestors from Ireland and – "

"Oh, superpowers, is it now," Rebecca interrupted. "Well, ain't dat da crac. Ya hear dat, Marty? Superpowers!" Marty chuckled without looking up. "All into your Irishness, is it?" Rebecca egged on. "An fearr leat an Ghaeilge?"

Dylan stared blankly at her without responding.

"I didn't think so," Rebecca stopped smiling. "The two of you aren't here to ask me questions. You're here because you're going to do something for me." She gave Anne a stern look. "Both of you."

"Then, this is the part where you tell us why you sent for us," Anne said curtly, "or we'll walk out of here and find someone else to help us."

"Do you like stories, Dylan?" Rebecca asked.

"I suppose, sure," he responded cautiously, legs crossed defensively.

"I was still a girl when my mother was burned alive. They started by flogging her near to death in the town square," Rebecca began. "They forced me to sit there and watch as the flesh was cleaved from her back, but as the blood trickled down her naked, limp body, something truly special happened. A tiny part of my mother's spirit – a small, sliver of her light – separated from her body. It circled around her while she moaned in agony, listless and confused, and then it came over to where I was sitting." Rebecca looked at Dylan, then back at Anne. "So, I just held out my hand. A simple thing, really. I just opened my palm and took the light from my mother. It was a very special day, for me. It was my mother's final lesson, her parting gift."

"So, you're a reaper?" Dylan asked.

"The next person who asks a question," Rebecca smacked her palm against the arm of the chair, "is going to spend the night in a small pine box, six feet underground, breathing through a straw!"

As Rebecca finished shouting the words, the room came alive with frantic whispers. Dylan and Anne exchanged a nervous glance as the familiar sound of anxious laughter circled their chairs.

"Awe, look, Marty," Rebecca taunted, "they've both gone pale." The voices faded as quickly as they had materialized. "Reapers are like Neanderthals, they just keep doing the same thing, the same way, no matter how much the world changes. I don't kill – at least, not anymore – because I've learned how to harness and take the light from others," she looked at Dylan and raised her eyebrow, "in much more enjoyable ways."

"Oh, fucking hell." Dylan grabbed his crotch. "Please stop!"

"That's enough!" Anne stood up and pushed the table over sideways so she could tower over Rebecca's chair. "Stop bullying him!" Anne looked down, her eyes blazing.

"Oh, now that is precious," Rebecca gave Anne a sideways glance. "Nancy didn't tell me the two of you had bonded." In an instant, Rebecca's hand went from the arm of the chair to Anne's throat. "Did you fuck him?" Her sparkling blue eyes turned black as coal.

"That's none of your bus—" Dylan started to say, then grimaced in pain.

Anne clawed at the hand around her throat and then spat defiantly in her captor's face.

"Clearly you haven't, which suits me perfectly." Rebecca wiped the spittle from her cheek with her free hand and then shoved Anne backwards into her chair. "Since the two of you know so little about your light, sex is the only way you could possibly bring your auras together. When two people with the light bond, their energies become connected, but they lose some of their power by giving themselves over to each other. I want all of your energy for myself, and it's so much better when I get to feed from raw, untouched innocence." She smirked at Dylan. "Martin, you're dismissed, but, be a dear and help Jessica fetch their things from their car before you leave."

Marty used his cane to stand up and shuffled out of the room without a word.

"Do you know they burned my mother on Samhain? You're familiar with Samhain, of course," Rebecca leaned against the wall and crossed her arms. She looked at Anne and then over at Dylan, who was still hunched over. "Halloween, Day of the Dead, yadda yadda. The time of year when the veil between the planes is thinnest, when our light is most powerful."

"Halloween is like a couple days from now," Dylan said.

"It's tomorrow," Anne corrected.

"The old ways were still very much alive back then, even though the true knowledge of the light was nearly gone." Rebecca waved her hand. "Of course, the official records added a few days, to avoid ecclesiastical criticism for burning a witch on such a glorious Pagan holiday, but the fires of Samhain burned a little brighter that day, I assure you. My mother's light came pouring out of the flames like a waterfall."

"But, what – I mean, why – no, where – it's Anne and I that," Dylan struggled with the words, trying not to group them into the form of a question.

"You're both here for a single reason," Rebecca said. "To go out to my circle on Samhain and feed me your energy. Supercharged by the crystal that was found in the cave under Nancy's hill, it will sustain me for decades, maybe centuries. Fact is, I don't actually know, and you're going to be my guinea pigs. But, I'm not a monster, so I'll give you a choice." She walked over so she was between Anne and Dylan, then leaned over and whispered softly into both of their ears, "You can either give it to me together, or I'll take it from you, one after the other."

"You disgust me," Anne said.

"Okay," Dylan whispered absently.

Rebecca was close enough that Dylan could smell the spicy musk of her breasts – dangling inches from his mouth – almost taste the salty sweetness of her flesh, and feel the firmness of her nipples on his tongue. His lap was rock hard, and his mind was consumed by a single, repetitive, thrusting thought. He didn't care if he had Rebecca alone, or her and Anne at the same time. He ached for the release she could provide.

"That's the spirit, little man," Rebecca took a small vial from a nearby shelf. She put a few drops of the thick red liquid on her finger and then ran it across Dylan's lips. He sucked at her finger passionately at first, then his breathing slowly returned to normal, and he regained his composure. Rebecca flicked Dylan's nose playfully. "That's better. I can't have you two spoiling all of my fun by hooking up before the big day." She glanced at Dylan's lap and then looked at Anne with narrow eyes. "He won't be able to get it up for weeks, so don't bother trying."

"Dylan!" Anne said and poked him in the shoulder.

"What?" he said and blinked. "What did I miss?"

"You're both my guests, for Samhain," Rebecca smiled and spread her arms invitingly. "I've got a little retreat out in the woods, built up on the property around my circle. I'd call it a compound, but that word makes me feel like a psycho. Fucking Branch Davidians."

Anne took Dylan by the hand as Rebecca leaned in again.

"Whaddya say we all take a little drive?"

CHAPTER SIXTEEN

Anne and Dylan sat in the backseat of Rebecca's black sedan and watched the world go by. The indifference of the concrete, flashing lights, blaring horns and frenzied pace of traffic slowly faded away. Eventually, they were alone, winding along two-lane roads through fields and forest. The world became one of striking contrast, the brownish red tint of slumbering leaves, and the soft beige of harvested crops languishing in the half-light of the Autumn sun. The fields and farms gradually gave in to the forest, and soon they were surrounded by trees. She knew they were driving north – more or less – but after five hours, she had no idea where the nearest town was, let alone what state they were in.

The road snaked through the countryside, and it was hard not to appreciate the beauty of the rocky granite cliffs that jutted out like ancient teeth against the thick red maw of the tree-lined river valley below. They turned onto a small two-track, and their ride began to jostle and slow even more. She and Dylan hadn't said anything since they were sitting in Rebecca's parlor, save for exchanging reassuring glances. Anne knew she wasn't alone in this, but Dylan seemed to be apologizing. His eyes were sympathetic; not scared, so much as sorry.

Anne didn't even realize they were holding hands until they came up to the entry gate to Rebecca's property, a classic testament of power and privilege made of stone and black iron. Jessica lowered her window, pushed a few buttons on a black console, and the gates separated so they could pass. The property was in the middle of a thick old-growth forest, but as they drove down the gravel driveway, lined with ancient yellow oaks, Rebecca's estate took shape. The driveway circled around a magnificent fountain of a young woman carrying a basket of flowers under one arm, with water pouring from the palm of her other elegantly outstretched hand. Even at the end of October, the fountain was surrounded by colorful flowers and herbs, vibrant and full of life.

The house tread a fine line between gothic and modern, a combination of stone and plaster that Anne had seen in her travels through Europe, but never on this scale. As they approached the house Anne's hand began to tingle, and she felt the familiar spark of their attraction. She took her hand away from Dylan's and her gaze was drawn to the small lake and the woods behind the palatial manor.

The stone circle stood nearby.

"You'd think I'd have more after 700 years," Rebecca said, "but it's been quite a challenge to stay under the radar." The car rolled to a stop and Anne stretched her sore limbs while Jessica retrieved their bags from the trunk. "Jessica will show you to your rooms - separate, I hope you don't mind. Who knows," she strode up the stone steps, "once I have some food in me, I might even answer some of your annoying questions."

Jessica led them inside, and Anne was immediately struck by how bright it was. Unlike the dark, gothic vibe of Rebecca's occult shop in Salem, the interior of her home was surprisingly modern, with white walls, and minimalist décor. Rebecca was already halfway up the oak staircase when Jessica motioned for them to follow. At the top of the stairs, Rebecca walked down the hallway, entered a room, then shut the door.

Jessica motioned the other direction, opened the first door, deposited Anne's bag, then opened the next door and deposited Dylan's.

"The dining room is directly below us, off the main foyer," she pointed to the floor. "Dinner is in an hour."

***

Rebecca was already eating when Anne and Dylan joined her in the dining room. She sat at the head of an enormous table big enough for twenty people. She stopped cutting her food long enough to gesture at the two spots next to her, one on each side, that were waiting for them. When they were seated, Jessica brought them each a plate from a warming station, and poured them a glass of wine.

"How are you feeling?" Dylan asked, then realized he had asked a question. "I mean, hey, Rebecca, what's, oh for, fuck's...can we ask you questions now?"

Rebecca looked at Dylan, chewed her food, and then took a long, slow drink of her wine. She gently set down the glass, then dabbed the corners of her mouth with her napkin.

"You have got to be the most adorable thing I've seen in decades," she said at last, then said to Anne, "don't you wanna just eat him up?" She picked up a carrot with her fingers and placed it in her mouth, sucking her fingertip seductively before she began to chew. "I'm going to have fun with you, tomorrow."

"Is that a yes, or a no?" Anne asked, unamused.

"Ask away," Rebecca waved her hand dismissively and started to cut the meat on her plate.

"Right," Anne began, "so don't you care? Don't you wanna know what happened? Complete the circle?"

"Complete the circle?" Rebecca stabbed a piece of meat with her knife and placed it in her mouth. "Who taught you that phrase, anyway? You couldn't possibly have any clue what that means," she said, talking around the food in her mouth. "How do you hope to complete anything?"

"Then, help us," Dylan said. "Your mother taught you things, didn't she tell you about the circle's true purpose?"

"You should try the venison, it's quite good." Rebecca looked at Dylan and lifted her eyebrow. "It's young, and tender."

"You're wrong," Anne said, "and would you please give it a rest? I am literally going to vomit all over you soon. Nancy and my grandfather gave me a book. It shows us the true purpose. It's all there in pictures, diagrams, and recipes. We're so close, Rebecca, we just need someone like you to fill in the gaps for us."

"You want me to teach you the secrets?" Rebecca asked Anne.

"Yeah, we just need some help, with, holy fucking Christ!" Anne grabbed the table with both hands and looked at Rebecca. "What are you doing to me?" Anne gasped for air, whimpered, then pounded the table with her fist. Her chest was on fire, and her entire body tingled with a mixture of anticipation, ecstasy and slow, measured release. "I did *not* give you permission to touch me like this!"

"You need to learn to keep your hands to yourself!" Dylan objected.

Rebecca sat up in her chair and gave Dylan a giddy smile, her eyes sparkling with glee.

"Listen to you," Rebecca said to Anne, "all modern and liberated. Women like you have always been the first to burn."

Anne's body relaxed and her breathing returned to normal, but her eyes dripped with venom.

"Why did you bring us here?" Anne seethed. "You don't actually think we'll just give ourselves to you for some crazy sex ritual, do you?"

"Sorry to disappoint you, but we're not having sex," Rebecca looked at Dylan. "But what we're going to share is deeply personal, and took me centuries to perfect."

"What does that mean?" Dylan asked.

"It means, I'm particular about who I invite over for dinner. You and Anne are descended from an especially powerful lineage. You're –"

"—Special?" Dylan rubbed his temples and closed his eyes. "Yeah, we got that part. We know that we were brother and sister like a thousand years ago, or something, but so far, nobody has explained what that means."

"Wait a minute," Anne said, regaining her composure. "It's you, isn't it? The woman from Ireland, the one that Dylan and I are descended from?"

"Like I said," Rebecca swallowed and smiled, "an especially powerful lineage."

"So, do you know about the book, or not?" Anne asked.

"I know all about your grandfather's book, Anne." Rebecca cocked her head and smiled, like a mother gazing upon a child. "It's a poor attempt to copy something I wrote myself about 300 years ago, when I still thought there was a chance to restore our people, and our purpose."

"So, help us," Dylan repeated. "Anne and I found each other for a reason. The diagrams in the book show a bright light coming out of the crystal in the capstone, and when I look at it, the stones form a three-dimensional shape, then I hear the phrase 'taganna dorchadas, eadrama solaras.' Do you know what that means?"

Rebecca stopped chewing and looked at Dylan.

"Taganna dorchadas, ead –" He started to repeat the phrase.

"—I heard you the first time," Rebecca interrupted.

She pulled out the velvet container with the crystal and propped it open on the table between Dylan and Anne's plates. As soon as she did, Dylan and Anne exchanged wide-eyed glances. It was glowing, just like Abigail's amulet had, and small waves of white light filled the room, radiating out from the crystal and onto their chests.

"I spent centuries chasing shadows, following rumors, and searching for this crystal. There was a time when I would have given anything to get my hands on it and complete the circle." Rebecca said. "The sacrifices I made, relationships I destroyed, promises I broke, all in the name of the knowledge I needed to write that book. You have no idea what those words mean, or what you're thinking about doing."

"Dr. Parsons," Anne said, "is working on understanding the layout of the stones and the carvings on the cave walls. If you talked to him, maybe we could figure this out, together? Maybe there are more crystals out there, too?"

"I don't need to see the wall of your cave to know what's there," Rebecca replied. "I've seen the patterned circles, and the two figures kneeling in the center in front of the capstone, in caves all over the world. How do you think I made those diagrams to begin with? The only reason your hill matters is that crystal. In almost 700 years, it's the only one I've come across." Rebecca stared longingly at the crystal in the center of the table. She reached out her hand and the light enveloped her fingertips in small, rippling waves. "Do you see how the light connects to us? The energy in the crystal is drawn to us, the same way that we're drawn to each other, and that's not a coincidence."

"How so?" Dylan asked.

"Taimid realtach," Rebecca said, her eyes suddenly fixed on a distant memory. "We're the light of the stars. And no, I don't really know what that means." She closed the velvet container and put the crystal back in her pocket. "What I do know, is that the things that made this crystal weren't from earth. The light they placed inside of us, and the knowledge of how to maintain the network of stone circles, disappeared thousands of years before I was born."

"But, Aislinn told us that –" Dylan started to say.

"—Aislinn," For a moment, Rebecca's eyes turned black, like a survival instinct had just been triggered, then quickly returned to normal. "You've met Aislinn?"

"Yeah," he replied, "she rescued us from a reaper on Anne's hill. She told us to stay together, and to keep looking for answers. She told us we could complete the circle."

"It's only one possible path for tomorrow, just one possible outcome," Rebecca said defensively, "and it's not the one that's going to play out."

"Come on, you're one of us," Dylan said exasperated. "Why won't you just help?"

"No, Dylan, I'm not like you – not anymore – and even if I knew the answers to all of your questions, I'm not about to let you use that crystal." Rebecca picked at her teeth with a long black fingernail, and then shoved her plate away. "The truth is that the light exists to feed the darkness, to sacrifice its energy to the vast, utter emptiness of the void. More to the point, *you're* going to feed *me*."

She pushed back her chair and stood up.

"Jessica will see to your needs," she said flatly and walked from the room.

Right on cue, Jessica filled Anne's glass again and set the bottle of wine on the table.

"Aren't you thirsty?" she asked Dylan, looking at his full glass.

"Oh, no, I," he looked at Anne. Somehow, he felt better knowing that she was aware of his past struggles. Rebecca was stronger than he was, stronger than them both, but seeing Anne sitting across the table from him gave Dylan a confidence he hadn't felt in a very long time. They were stronger together, just like Aislinn said. "No, I don't drink, but I'd love some water." Jessica walked into the kitchen and returned with a carafe of ice water, filled an empty glass for Dylan, and set the carafe on the table. "So, how long have you worked for Rebecca?" he asked.

"We met in London, right after Queen Victoria was crowned."

"Okay, I know that was a while ago," Dylan said and took a drink of water. "But when exactly was that again?"

"It was the summer of 1838," Jessica smiled. "She stole my heart, and I taught her how to love again. I don't work for Rebecca, we're together."

"No offense," Anne said, "but you seem to be doing all of the work in this relationship."

"It's true," Jessica said, "we do have a domestic arrangement, but I don't mind. Rebecca cares for me, provides for me, and I do it gladly."

"How does that work, exactly?" Dylan asked. "Not the part where you're both women," he added quickly, "I mean, she's kind of a reaper. Are you a reaper, too?"

"No," Jessica said, "I don't harvest anything from anyone. Rebecca sustains me by sharing herself with me, giving me some of the light she takes from others."

"So, you have the light?" Dylan asked and she nodded.

"Wow, forever young," Anne narrowed her eyes, "As long as you have a steady supply of house guests to keep Rebecca's tank full, I guess you're all set."

"If you need anything, I'll be in the front room reading until midnight," Jessica said. "After that, you can find me in our bedroom at the end of the hall."

Jessica walked from the room.

"That was awkward," Dylan said.

"This whole thing is awkward," Anne said, cutting her meat.

"Rebecca clearly doesn't understand personal boundaries," Dylan said, "but did you see the look on her face when she left?"

"I know, it's like she gave up at some point. That must be why my grandfather never gave me the whole story, because he knew it would just lead me to her," Anne drained her wine and slammed her glass on the table. "Dylan, I think we can do this, I think we can beat her. I say we go into that circle tomorrow and do our thing. Complete it, or whatever the fuck."

"That's what I'm talking about!" Dylan clapped his hands and pounded the table. "But we still don't know what that means, do we?"

"Not yet," Anne took another bite of food and filled her glass again, "but she's hiding something. It's in that book, and I'm going to find it. Fucking, touch me like that? Oh, it's on." Anne chewed vigorously, and took another drink of wine, her eyes burning with determination. "She gave up, but we don't have to."

Anne's mood didn't improve as they finished their meal. Rebecca's obstinance and the unanswered questions were bad enough, but the wine seemed to be fueling Anne's agitation.

"Maybe we should go check out Rebecca's circle," Dylan suggested. "You know, maybe it will help us *figure it out.*" He mouthed the final words silently and nodded repeatedly toward the door.

Anne giggled and agreed.

The front door was unlocked, and Anne stopped as they walked past the fountain. She bent down, took a couple of deep breaths and ran her fingers through the herbs and flowers.

"I read about Airmid while we were on the plane," she said. "Apparently, she discovered all of the healing herbs in the known world."

"No kidding," Dylan said.

"Yeah, they grew from her brother's grave," Anne continued, "watered by her tears as she mourned his death."

"Ugh," Dylan said in mock protest. "Don't you know any happy stories?"

"I'm just saying," Anne stood up again, "it's hard not to think there's some truth to legends and folk tales. When I look at this garden, I can't help but think there's something supernatural going on. Rebecca's obviously called Airmid for a reason."

Dylan looked at the flowers briefly and then tugged at Anne's shirt.

"Come on," he said.

They continued onto a gravel path that hugged the lakeshore, with lampposts lighting the way, following it until it split off into the forest. The air was crisp and the night sky was blanketed with stars. Dylan took Anne's hand and felt the warmth of her touch surge up his arm.

"That feels good," Anne said. "It's chilly tonight."

Dylan and Anne both stopped as they came into Rebecca's circle, waiting for their eyes to adjust to the darkness. Unlike the stones on Anne's hill, which were scattered and broken, Rebecca's was pristine. The stones were upright, spaced out evenly in a perfect circle, and someone had even removed all of the fallen leaves from the immaculately maintained grass.

"Look," Anne said using her phone as a flashlight, "the runes from the amulet are carved into the stones, just like in the book."

Dylan stood in front of the capstone and motioned for Anne to join him. He took her in his arms and cradled her head against his shoulder. The energy wrapped around them and Anne was immediately soothed. With each passing moment, she felt her head clear and the lingering frustration from dinner faded away.

"We're stronger together," Anne looked at him, confirming Dylan's feelings. "It's like Aislinn said, we should stay together."

"Rebecca was genuinely afraid when I mentioned Aislinn," Dylan said. "It's like she knows that we're different, that there's a legit chance we can actually do this."

"The way she was talking, it sounds like she has the vision, too," Anne said.

"You think she's seen us complete the circle?" Dylan asked.

"I don't know," Anne buried her head again and hugged him tightly, "but if we're going to beat her at her own game, we've got less than 24 hours to figure it out."

***

Back in her room, tucked into the softest blanket she had ever felt, and wrapped up in sheets with a thread count she had never experienced, Anne looked through her grandfather's book – Rebecca's book, as it turned out – and looked for answers. If Anne's hunch was correct, Rebecca wrote the book while she still cared, when she still thought there was hope to restore the old ways.

She flipped to the diagram with the two kneeling figures and ran her fingers across the stones. There must be a pattern, something that could betray Rebecca's stoic denial, and her resignation to the darkness. She flipped to the diagram for the Samhain ritual, and looked again at the kneeling figures, the light coming out from the capstone, and the symbols on the page. She ran her finger across the page and noticed a dark puddle next to the male figure, with a small stream flowing away to one of the stones.

Anne flipped to the diagram for midsummer and looked at the kneeling figures. There was no puddle, no stream. She flipped to both equinoxes and again, nothing. They were only on the diagram for

Samhain. She looked at the stone that the stream led to, examined the symbol and gasped.

She knew what it meant.

She knew what would happen.

***

"It's time," someone called from the edge of the stones. "Complete the circle."

The chanting echoed in the fog of Dylan's dream, as he and his companion entered the circle.

Dylan took her by the hand and a cold heat surged up his arm and into his chest. They walked together to the far end of the stones, where the capstone glowed bright white. They knelt, his left hand laced tightly into her right and they said the words together.

"Taganna dorchadas, eodrama solaris."

The drums beat louder, and they repeated the phrase over and over, the energy in his chest growing hotter. Dylan looked down and saw the white pulsing light arc outward from his chest to the glowing capstone. The markings on the stones around them began to glow red, pulsing in rhythm with the stone amulet she wore around her neck, and he noticed her voice for the first time.

He looked into Mary's soft blue eyes as she repeated the words, over and over, until the circle and Dylan's dream were consumed by the brightness.

CHAPTER SEVENTEEN

Dylan woke up the next day, still excited from his dream. Seeing Mary in the circle was a sign, it had to be. He threw on his clothes, walked across the hall, and knocked on Anne's door. When she opened it, the words burst from his mouth.

"I had a dream last night," he said, "I know what we have to do, and I know it will work."

"I figured it out," she said excitedly. "Wait, what?"

"The circle," Dylan said. "I know how to complete it, to open a portal. We can do this, Anne, I know we can. The crystal in the capstone creates some sort of link with me, and then from me to you because of that amulet you found."

"Dylan, no," Anne walked over to the table next to her bed and retrieved the book. "Look, right here." She pointed to the diagram. "Look at the dark puddle, and the stream running away from it. Do you see that?"

"Yeah, so what?"

"So, none of the other diagrams have that, that's so what." She pointed at the stone. "Do you see that symbol?"

"Fuck, just tell me, already!"

"Death!" Anne shoved the book into Dylan's arms. "I think that's a pool of blood, and that's the symbol for death!"

"Whoa," Dylan said and looked at the diagram again. "How do you know that? I thought we didn't know what these symbols meant."

"I just know," Anne said, exasperated. "How did you know about the three-dimensional shapes and that secret password?"

"It just kind of popped into my head."

"Well, I look at this symbol and I see death." Anne grabbed Dylan's t-shirt and pulled him close. "I'm not going to be part of something that ends with you dying, I can't," she looked away surprised by the power of her emotion. "I know we barely know each other, but I can't say goodbye to you. Not so soon, and *definitely* not like this."

"Maybe it's just because it's Samhain," Dylan said and looked at the diagram. "You know, Day of the Dead, when the veil is the thinnest, yadda-yadda."

Anne laughed and buried her head in his shoulder.

"Please, I'm serious. Let's just give ourselves to Rebecca and be done with it," Anne pleaded. "She can take what she wants, just like she did with your uncle, and then you and I can get on with our lives." She kissed him on the cheek. "Together."

They both turned around as Jessica knocked on the door frame.

"Sorry about the subterfuge, but it's nearly time."

"Holy shit," Anne noticed the time on the clock for the first time. "It's four-o-clock in the afternoon."

"Yeah, Rebecca might have had me spike the wine last night," Jessica responded. "And the water. Again, real sorry, but she wanted to make sure you were well rested for the ritual. There are gowns in your closets that she'd like you to wear, for ceremonial reasons and, uh, ease of access."

"We're not changing into anything," Dylan said.

"Oh, he's just kidding," Anne tittered and then said to Dylan, "we'd be delighted to wear the gowns."

"I'm not wearing a gown."

"We're wearing the gowns."

"You know, it really doesn't matter, she's going to get what she wants," Jessica said, confused by the sudden tension, "but it will go better for all of us if you just wear the gowns."

"I'm not, wearing, a gown."

"Dylan!" Anne said through a forced smile.

"Either way, it's time to get dressed," Jessica pointed, and Dylan went into his room across the hall.

Anne threw her clothes into a pile on the bed, retrieved the black satin gown from the closet, and put it on. She brushed out her hair, and let it fall across her shoulder. She touched up her eyeliner and mascara, applied the black lipstick that Rebecca had left for her, and then fastened the robe. She took the amulet from the leather pouch and ran her finger across the shimmering stones.

Shit, she thought and secured the amulet around her neck.

She walked out the door and into the hallway.

Jessica was waiting patiently, wearing an identical black gown. Anne's heart sank when she saw Dylan leaning against the wall across from her. He was still wearing black jeans, a black t-shirt, and black Converse tennis shoes.

She started to protest again, but Jessica motioned them to follow.

"It's time," she said and led them down the stairs. "Rebecca is waiting for us."

Dylan took her hand, and the spark of their connection coursed up her arm.

"Come on," he said quietly, "we got this."

They walked down the gravel path next to the lake, the lampposts already flickering against the late afternoon sun. They followed Jessica into the forest where a large bonfire was roaring in the center of the circle. Rebecca spread out her arms in welcome.

"Thanks for volunteering to go first," she said to Anne. "I promise, I'll be gentle. But you, naughty boy," she looked Dylan up and down. "I'm going to have some fun with you."

Rebecca turned around and walked toward the capstone at the end of the circle.

"Once the crystal is activated, follow my lead," Dylan whispered to Anne.

"Dylan, no," Anne pleaded. "please don't do this."

Rebecca put the crystal into the shallow depression of the capstone and Anne felt an immediate surge of energy course through her body.

The amulet around Anne's neck began to shimmer a rainbow of colors, and the ancient symbols on the stones around them burned red. Rebecca turned around to face Dylan and Anne, lifted her arms and the air began to hum. She shrugged her shoulders and her black gown fell to the ground in a heap.

Dylan's eyes were glued to her naked form, as if in a trance, and Anne also found herself drenched in a simmering desire that warmed her body and lingered in her chest. The tattoo of the black and red serpent was much larger than it appeared, slithering around Rebecca's entire body, the wooden stake running the length of her torso, from her sternum to just below her belly button. The heat grew stronger, surging with every beat of her heart.

Rebecca walked over to Anne and untied her gown. She slowly ran her hands up the silk fabric, stroked her hair and kissed her gently on the lips. Anne's body was on fire, every inch of her flesh, every cell, alive with the heat of Rebecca's touch. Anne gave Dylan a guilty look, but he just stood next to them and stared, as if unable to move.

The mischievous smile on Rebecca's face faded in an instant as the energy in the circle around them began to change. Instead of the raw electricity of their mutual bond, the air began to hum with the frenzied whispers of a reaper. The air swirled like a tornado, scattering the leaves at the edge of the circle all around them. Rebecca turned around just as Aislinn appeared near the capstone.

"You," Rebecca's face went pale. "Why are you here?"

"You know this can't happen," she said to Rebecca.

"No," Rebecca said, "it doesn't have to be the end." She looked at Jessica. "Please, just a little longer."

"This time is over," Aislinn looked at Anne and Dylan. "They're from your line, but they also have the knowledge that you lack. They're the key, they can reverse the path and restore what was."

"But I don't want them to," Rebecca moved closer to Dylan and Anne and held out her arms protectively. The snake painted on Rebecca's body began to move, coiled up in anticipation and hissed at Aislinn. "They're mine!"

Rebecca looked nervously around as her shout reverberated against the trees. The forest came alive with the howls of tortured souls and angry laughter, and another swirling black vortex rushed into the circle, extinguishing the bonfire and throwing embers in every direction.

"Becky!" Jessica screamed and ran to Rebecca's side.

"You, fucking cunt!" Rebecca yelled at Aislinn and dropped to her knees. "You did this! You brought them down on us, didn't you?" Rebecca grabbed the side of her head and shrieked, her body convulsing.

Twilight was consumed by darkness, as a second and third reaper descended upon the circle. Aislinn rushed past Dylan and Anne, drawing her swords and shrieking into the darkness beyond what was left of the bonfire to meet her newly arrived foes.

"Now!" Dylan grabbed Anne's arm. "We have to finish it, while we still can!"

He tugged on her arm and began to run toward the capstone, but Anne resisted.

"Dylan, no," Anne look around at the dark scene unfolding around her, and she hesitated. "If we complete the circle, you'll die. I'm not – "

"If you don't, we'll both die!" he shouted and started for the capstone.

Anne felt a wave of raw heat from the other end of the stones, every sound was sucked out of the hill, and suddenly Dylan was running to the capstone in slow motion. His body was silhouetted against the light pulsing from the capstone, with yellow and orange leaves suspended around him.

The world stuttered, resumed its normal pace, and then completely fell apart.

Dylan disappeared in a blinding flash of light, and Rebecca howled in anguish, writhing on the ground while Jessica screamed beside her, before finally imploding into the darkness.

A clap of thunder rolled through the hills surrounding the stone circle, and again Anne was left only with the ringing in her ears. Jessica was gone, and now she was running in slow motion, looking for Dylan and trying to shout into the soundless void.

Time resumed and Anne's shouts came alive, but in the next moment, came shrieking to a halt, and she was pinned against one of the stones at the perimeter of the circle. She watched helplessly, as Dylan's chest exploded slowly in a blinding flash of light.

She got to her knees as time flowed again.

"Dylan!"

Anne's body coursed with energy, and she felt the power of the crystal behind her growing in unison with the heat of the amulet around her neck. Something deep inside Anne was begging to be let go. A pulse of light rippled from her chest and cut through the darkness, displacing the swirling black mass attacking Dylan, and clearing a path to where he lay on the ground.

Aislinn stumbled into the far end of the circle, dropped to one knee, and used her one remaining sword like a crutch to support her mangled torso. She shouted defiantly as the swirling vortex surrounded her. Anne reached Dylan and knelt beside him, taking his head into her arms and wiping the blood from the corner of his mouth. He was conscious, but blood was pouring from the hole in his chest and the gash across his shoulder.

"Please," Dylan said, coughing up more red liquid. "I know what this means, I know what will happen, I know..." His eyes rolled backward, and his head went limp in Anne's arms.

Anne was consumed by raw emotion – rage, doubt, fear and regret mingled with her courage – and she screamed. From the bottom of her gut, the depths of her soul, she shared her primal shout with the universe.

But there was no sound.

The blood pulsing from Dylan's chest stopped moving, and the lazy red track dripping from the corner of his mouth was suspended in midair.

The world around her was filled with a rich, velvety hail of dark shrapnel. Even without sound and the flow of time, Anne knew that Aislinn was gone, and that she would have to face the last reaper alone.

With a grating hiss, time slipped back into place and Anne's shriek finally filled the stone circle. Her energy created a sphere of light where she sat and cradled Dylan's head in her lap. The final reaper closed in, and they were surrounded by the darkness of the void. Anne knew the battle was over, and she finally understood that running away had never been an option. She knew she wasn't alone, that she needed to do her part, so she let go. She let go and she let Dylan in.

"Taganna dorchadas, eadrama solaras," Anne whispered and kissed Dylan on the forehead. "Taganna dorchadas, eadrama solaras," she hissed loudly at the darkness around her.

"Taganna dorchadas, eadrama solaras!"

She cradled Dylan's head against her chest and rocked back and forth, shouting the phrase over and over. As she did, the entire circle was bathed in a brilliant blue light and a deep pulse of energy was released in all directions, traveling out to the horizon and beyond. The last reaper shrieked and disintegrated, melting into a misty vapor that was consumed by the intensity of the light. Anne continued to shout her intentions into the canopy of trees as the energy around her continued to grow, shook the ground, and blanketed the forest in a deafening roar.

Anne looked up and screamed as she and Dylan were consumed by the light.

***

As the light faded, Dylan's surroundings slowly came into focus. His spirits sank as he recognized the walls of shimmering light and gnarly roots of the room beneath the willow tree.

Whatever he and Anne did, it didn't work.

His fears were confirmed when Abigail walked out of the light, hand-in-hand with Constance and Margaret. Dylan forced himself into a sitting position, but stayed on the ground, his forehead supported by the palm of his right hand.

"What happened?" he asked without looking up.

"You didn't tell me you were going back to the hill with Anne," Abigail said. "When I last saw you two, you were going your separate ways. Not that it would have mattered, I guess, but what exactly were you hoping to accomplish?"

Margaret started to giggle, but Constance elbowed her and put a finger to her lips.

"You know what I wanted," Dylan replied. "I wanted to open a gate to the outer realms, whatever that means." He finally looked up at Abigail and the girls and took a deep breath. "You know why I did it, but clearly, it didn't work. Wait, did you say back to the hill? What are you talking about?"

"Now, Mommy?" Margaret asked.

"Yes, now is fine," Abigail looked down at Margaret and smiled.

"Here, Mr. Ward," she said and handed him a single white flower. "I picked this for you to say thank you."

"Thank you?" Dylan asked. "For what?"

"For giving us a new home," she said. "I have new friends and a whole new world to explore and the forest, oh, Mr. Ward, the forest is so big! Will you please play hide-and-seek with me in the forest?"

"Whoa, slow down," Dylan looked at Abigail. "I don't understand."

"It worked, silly," Abigail kissed Dylan on the forehead.

The white light at the edges of the room shimmered and then faded, revealing a lush green meadow, where butterflies every color of the rainbow danced among white and purple flowers. They were on the edge of a forest, with enormous trees that grew straight up into the air before stretching their arms sideways into a vibrant green canopy. On the ground, more familiar looking trees flourished, their twisted, ancient trunks curling back on themselves into friendly shapes that seemed to be saying hello.

"See?" Margaret said and pointed at the trees. "I have the best spot picked out! You're never gonna find me!" She tugged on Abigail's arm. "Can we play now, Mommy, please?"

"In a minute, sweetheart," Abigail said. "Mr. Ward needs some time to get used to our new home." She smiled at Dylan and raised her arms in the air. "You did open a portal, Dylan," she said, "and it set us free – us and countless of our kindred spirits."

"It worked…" Dylan said and looked around.

White and red light streaked by in all directions, converging at a large city off in the distance that was perched on the edge of a vast blue ocean. The city grew right out of the earth, an organic network of vegetation with five mountainous pillars that rose into the sky.

"So, where are we?"

"Not so much where, as when," Abigail replied, "but I think there's someone who would love to answer all your questions."

A white light hovered above Dylan's head and then floated gently to the ground in front of him. The light shimmered briefly, then Mary appeared, smiling, her arms outstretched. Dylan quickly closed the distance between their bodies and buried his face in her soft, black hair.

"Am I dead?" he asked without letting go.

"Your soul is in stasis," Mary said, "which is why you're able to be here with me, Dylan – here, in this special place – for those that carry the light."

"Wait, you have it, too?" Dylan asked.

Mary nodded her head.

"So, this is the future?" Dylan looked around again. "What is stasis? I don't understand."

"One possible future, yes," Mary replied, "with parts of the past mixed in. It's how we wanted it to be, it's what we chose. You and Anne created a portal, but you also cleansed that plane from the darkness, and finally made it possible for all of us to come home."

"Anne," Dylan was surprised how strongly his heart ached for her. "Is she alright? Is she alive?"

"Yes, she's fine," Mary said, "but that's what I mean by stasis. You have a choice to make. There are many possible futures for you and Anne, but they all depend on what you decide right now. You can return to her, or you can stay here."

"You've gotta be fucking kidding me! We literally just saved the universe, and you're telling me that I have another life altering choice to make?" Dylan took Mary by the hands. "What about our love? What about us?"

"What about us," Mary replied. "I told you, the love we shared when I was alive will never change, but things are different here. Some souls have many common destinies, and multiple soulmates." She looked at Abigail, who blushed and busied herself with helping the girls pick flowers. "When you're free of your physical bonds, when you completely move on, you'll see that the universe is different, that relationships can have deeper, richer meaning, and that time isn't measured by a single lifetime."

"So, wait," Dylan raised an eyebrow, "you and Abigail?"

"Not just Abigail," Mary replied, "but yes, she and I do have a common destiny and we've even shared a couple lifetimes together. Abigail and I go back to the beginning, to when the light first arrived on earth. It's only because you completed the circle that we were able to rebuild this place, and when we did, our collective consciousness was restored. We were sisters. She was Airmid and I was Edain."

"Abigail was Airmid?" Dylan sighed and rubbed his forehead. "I don't know, maybe I'm not ready for this, yet. What exactly is this place, anyway?"

"It's a waypoint," she said, "a place for bright souls to recharge before they journey on to other places in the outer realms, or return to the lower planes to continue their work."

"So, there are more places like this?"

"Many thousands."

"And how many planets are there like earth?"

"You don't want to know," Mary smiled sympathetically. "It wouldn't help your headache. Let's keep it simple – in order to complete the circle, you had to let go of your feelings for me. You had to learn to trust again, to let go of the past, and to stand together with Anne?"

"Yes."

"You didn't save the universe by yourself. It took both of you to complete the circle, and what you have, what you feel with Anne, is real," Mary said. "Anne's feelings for you are also real, and the chance for two bright souls to share their lives, as the universe intended? Now, that, is a very special thing."

"But everything's gonna be okay, right?" Dylan asked. "I mean, we did it? We fixed the glitch, or whatever?"

"What you did was only the beginning," Mary said. "You helped complete something that was stopped thousands of years ago, but tomorrow's path still depends on what you decide. If you go back, you and Anne will need to carry on the work that you've started. You'll need to teach others about the healing powers of the hill, and help restore balance through the collective consciousness that makes the stone circles so special. It's your choice."

Now that he was finally here, and Mary was standing in front of him, Dylan was completely conflicted. All he had to do was say the words and he could stay here with her in paradise and become part of the mystical workings of the universe. But she wasn't the same, and he wouldn't be the same, especially since he met Anne. Their connection was different – yes, it was new, mysterious and intriguing – but it was also stronger.

When Dylan looked into Anne's eyes he felt a comfort that he'd never experienced before, not even with Mary.

Dylan looked down as Maggie pulled on his shirt. She waved her hand, so he bent over and turned his head to the side, while she got up on her tiptoes.

"It's okay," she whispered into his ear, "if you'd rather, we can play tomorrow."

Dylan looked at Mary and said the words that were in his heart.

***

Anne stirred as the light faded.

She was still inside the stone circle, lying next to Dylan, but they were on her grandfather's hill, overlooking Lake Huron. Dylan was on his back, eyes open and unblinking, staring into the sky above the trees. She raised herself up onto an elbow and touched him with her other hand. The spark was gone.

"Dylan, wake up!" Anne got to her knees and shook his shoulders with both hands, but he didn't respond. "Dylan!" She shouted and pounded his chest with her fists. Anne looked down at her shaking hands, now red with his blood, and she knew he was gone. She wiped her hands on the ground and looked around at the stone circle. "Why...why did you insist on doing this?"

Anne started to cry, gently at first, but then she buried her head in what was left of Dylan's chest and she sobbed uncontrollably. A few weeks ago, Anne didn't even know that Dylan existed, but now she wondered if the hill – her life – would ever be the same. Now that she knew the hill's true purpose, she couldn't imagine it without him.

As Anne wiped away her tears, the hill came alive, shimmering with a fine veil of bright light. The crystal in the capstone pulsed and Dylan's body began to glow with a soft, blue light. Anne watched as he started to shimmer, and the hole in his chest began to rebuild itself, closed and then healed completely.

"Shit," Anne whispered to herself.

As soon as the words left her mouth, Dylan sat straight up and gasped for air.

"Fucking hell, that hurts!" He croaked and rubbed his chest.

Anne's eyes got wide, and for a moment she hesitated, like she wasn't sure if it was really happening.

"Dylan?" She touched his cheek and he smiled. "Dylan!"

Anne pounced, and Dylan hit the ground with a grunt, followed quickly by a muffled groan. Anne straddled his waist, grabbed him with both hands and ran her fingers through his hair. Anne's body came alive, and a ripple went up her spine and into her chest, as the warmth of their connection was reestablished. Dylan did his best to respond in kind, but it wasn't until he whimpered that Anne remembered what had just happened.

"What's going on?" She got to her feet and helped Dylan stand up. "You were dead! You bled out on the ground in front of the capstone. Are you okay?"

"Yeah, I think so," he said. "There's a lot I need to tell you, but it worked. We did it, we made some sort of portal, and I was in the outer realms."

"Seriously?" Anne said. "Well, it looks like we took care of the reapers, too."

"What about you?" Dylan asked. "You've got blood all over you. Are you hurt?"

"No, I'm fine," Anne wiped her face with her hands. "That's your blood, you idiot."

"Oh, right."

"What's that?" Anne asked and pointed.

Dylan held up a single white flower.

"This is for you."

Tell-Tale would like to thank you for your purchase. If you would like to read more by this or other fine TT authors, please visit our website: www.tell-talepublishing.com

www.ingramcontent.com/pod-product-compliance
Lightning Source LLC
Chambersburg PA
CBHW050407190726
48284CB00007BB/2463

* 9 7 8 1 9 5 2 0 2 0 0 5 6 *